IN SEARCH OF

OF

JEREMY

GRIFFIN

D0967740

A NOVEL BY

JACQUELINE

OPRESNIK

ISBN 978-1-7753752-1-0   book
ISBN 978-1-7753752-2-7   e-book

Cover designed by Sandra Muzyka

Dedication:

For Marjorie, whose memory of a young girl standing by the kitchen door, inspired me to write this novel.

Other Books
by Jacqueline Opresnik

The Misha Plate
Package From the Past
The Grants of Maxwell Street
The Grants at War
The Hunt for William Williamson

Chapter 1

"I was about seven." Hannah Wentworth's aged hands clutched the picture of her grandparents, the frame worn and faded. "They were in the kitchen; my grandparents, and my uncle Jo. They were arguing, and my uncle was very upset. He was yelling at my grandfather."

Tessa watched as the older woman's mind went back to the year 1927. Her memory not diminished by her ninety-eight years. Her face grimaced with the memory. "They thought I was in bed, but the noise had wakened me. My mother was with them too. Then I heard my grandmother raise her voice. She said to my grandfather, 'How could you leave your child? You should never have left Jeremy behind.' After that I heard the door slam and my uncle Jo left. I never saw him again." She paused, her emotions suddenly showing; the sadness at a family fractured by something she didn't understand.

"No one ever mentioned the argument"—she smiled ruefully— "at least not in front of me. I did think that something must have happened to this Jeremy. Perhaps they knew where he was and that he had died." Her eyes closed in thought.

Her hair was peppered grey, not the white you would

associate with a woman of her years. Her eyes were bright, and she seemed genuinely pleased to meet Tessa.

Hannah Wentworth was rich, very rich. And with no heirs she was the last of her grandfather's line –unless Tessa could find Jeremy Griffin.

"You realize he's probably" –there was no way to be delicate and she wondered if the older woman had realized how much time had elapsed since 1927— "passed on by now."

A servant knocked gently upon the library door and entered with a tray of tea and biscuits. She sat the tray down on a small table that had been placed between Tessa and Hannah Wentworth. She silently poured the tea for both leaving it to Tessa to add her own milk and sugar while she prepared Hannah's tea to her liking. Hannah waited until the servant left before continuing. She took her first sip, contemplating the enormous task she was asking.

Her eyes saddened then softened. "Yes. But he may have had family and I want them to share in his father's wealth. Maybe he never knew my grandfather was his father. I don't know who raised him or what happened to him, but he deserves to … I mean his family deserve to know his people … their people." She looked down at the photo, her aging years suddenly taking hold of her, and she closed her eyes.

It had been a hectic day. Called into her boss's office, Tessa had been briefed on the job she would be taking on and given papers to read to familiarize herself with her potential client. Tessa had worked for her investigative firm for two years now. She was the junior member on staff and when her boss found out Hannah Wentworth's request involved a man from 1880, he was more than relieved to give the investigation to Tessa, sensing nothing would come of it and regarding the elderly woman as senile. After all her lawyer was a good friend of his and had told him as much.

Coming away from the briefing Tessa had sat at her desk going over everything their office had on file. There were no scandals to speak of. It seemed the family kept a low profile. There were of course, stories about the new heiress but not much more. Hannah Wentworth was worth over seventy-eight million dollars. She was the only child of Isabel Wentworth who had been one of three children of Cyrus Thomas Griffin. Hannah's Uncle Jo had been the eldest son but had died in 1933, in India, unmarried and childless. His second son Wil had been married and had a son named Henry who had died on a bombing mission in World War Two. His parents had died the year before in the Blitz.

After leaving Devon, her grandfather had remarried and had a daughter by this union; Hannah's mother Isabel. Cyrus had provided for his family but had left his fortune to his only granddaughter–Hannah.

Now there was possibly a fourth child, or so it seemed from the conversation Hannah had heard when she was seven. And it was Tessa's job to find him and if they existed—his family.

Tessa had taken a cab to Hannah's Niagara-on-the-Lake address, a large century home near the lake, modest compared to today' s mansions but still large and stately for one person. Now she was sitting with this impressive person and hoped she could help her find the missing Jeremy. Their short visit had exhausted the older woman.

"You're tired. We can talk again tomorrow."

After making another appointment with Hannah's long-time butler Duffy, Tessa picked up her recorder and note book then left to begin her hunt. Where to start? This was her third missing persons case she had worked on but never one a hundred years old. Searching for a man born in 1880 so you could give his family a fortune seemed a difficult task, if indeed he had grown, married and had a family and for

Hannah's sake she hoped he had.

She would have to start with Hannah's family and work her way back. Her first thought was to hire a genealogist, but she was also determined to find this person on her own.

Genealogy was never a tool she thought she would need in hunting for missing people and it was one she knew little about but one she might have to learn about if she was to solve this case.

Should be simple enough. She would search on a genealogical site that showed British census records and go from there. She was aware that she would need the actual documentation not just the on-line records but that was a place to start, she could get the actual records later.

For any investigation results to be valid she must prove the family link between Cyrus Thomas Griffin and his lost son Jeremy before looking into Jeremy's descendants, if any. So, she would start by tracing the family back through the available census records to a time just after Jeremy's birth-1881. Once found she could then verify the family's location, then find the child's birth and baptism records as well as his parents marriage record, then go from there and search for Jeremy through the years while also adding the verified records of his life and his children.

There had to be more than a couple of genealogical sites available on line so first she Googled and was rewarded with several popular research sites. She chose Ancestry to begin with because they had a fourteen-day free trial. Scanning the available subscriptions Tessa picked the one with the most coverage. After giving her information and registering she began hunting for Cyrus Thomas Griffin in the 1911 census. From Hannah she had some pertinent facts. She knew Cyrus Thomas Griffin's date of birth, so she would start there. She typed in the lengthy name, born 1854, in Devon for the census records for 1911.

It didn't take long for the family members to pop up on the census page. Cyrus T. Griffin lived on Piccadilly Road with his wife Emily and his daughter by his new wife; Isabel. Isabel's two step- brothers were absent, obviously of an age to be on their own. She noticed the posh address, ages of the family members listed, and his occupation written as, employer of 310 men. She printed out a copy of the record.

She was surprised how detailed the 1911 census record was. Besides the usual name, age, occupation, and birthplace, the census record also disclosed how long the couple had been married as well as to the number of children born within this union, whether still living or dead. In her notebook she noted the main information and folded the printed copy, placing it in the back of her book for reference.

Next, she'd check the 1901 census. Once again, the requested name came up on the top of the first page. This time the address was different. The family was living on a street off Piccadilly Road. Regent Street was still a well-off area and the head of the household was described as living on own means which in 1901 meant simply compared to others, he was well off. The family dynamics were the same listing the younger child and his new wife. Again, Tessa printed a copy of the census record.

She felt confident that her search would go well. She went back to the main search page and plugged in the information for the 1891 census. Again, the family came up much as before living also on Regent Street. His new wife and this time all three children were listed. Jo was listed as an office clerk's assistant. Wil was shown as a messenger. Isabel, still a young child was in school. She was making progress and looked forward to finding out about the family dynamics on the '81 census.

Again, she entered the required information into the search criteria, then pressed the gold search button. She looked forward to seeing the two boys, aged four and two and for the first time, the baby Jeremy who would be approximately a year or less in age and waited for the list of results to appear. Unlike the previous searches in the later years the family was not among the families listed. Tessa looked at the next two pages and still nothing. Then she went back to edit the search information to make sure she hadn't made a mistake with the years. Cyrus Griffin age twenty-seven, born Devon, England. Everything was correct as it had been for the later years, so she pressed search again, and again nothing.

So, Tessa widened the search. She increased the age to include ten years before and after the 1854 year and included all of England instead of just Devon. Confident, she pressed the search button expecting to see the family at the top of the page—nothing. Next, she tried looking for the sons of Cyrus and searched independently for Joseph and William. She checked the census records for the boys' names and ages hoping to find them together with the right family. There were a few with each name but none in Devon and none with the family members she was looking for. For the next hour she tried looking for a first marriage for Cyrus. By eleven o'clock she was getting tired and had found nothing that might indicate the family had lived in England. Why would a man with three young children, one of which was an infant, leave the country?

It was late, and she was no closer to finding Jeremy Griffin.

Chapter 2

The building was small but had three floors; the uppermost, housing the library's family history collection. It was midday and most of the patrons were exploring the library's literary offers of the first two floors. As the elevator stopped at the third, she noticed a volunteer librarian sitting at a small desk opposite the elevator doors. He was an elderly man and seemed absorbed in a book he was reading as she approached his desk. He smiled, eager to answer questions from a fellow enthusiast no matter how amateur in nature. After explaining her missing Devon family, he directed her to the Devon section suggesting she might start with prominent Devon families.

The shelving was not as high as most libraries she'd been in and between open books decorating the flat shelf surface she could see the entire third floor over the top. The only other patron was a tall young man two shelving units away. He seemed engrossed in a book he had open and was reading. As if sensing her there he glanced up from his book and looked her way, giving a faint smile of recognition to a fellow searcher.

There were three books relating to families in Devon,

so she pulled these from the shelf and set them in the small buggy provided to patrons for book collecting. There were two books written to help the amateur genealogist, explaining how to track down ancestors. She would take those too, if only to verify she was on the right track. She would stay a while reading her choices, and then only check out the books she felt might help her further. She took a place at the end of the table deciding to look up the Devon families in the first book chosen.

"Do you mind if I share your table?" said the young man she had seen a few moments before.

She glanced down the length of the long table whose chairs on either side had remained empty since her arrival. She smiled. "Not at all." She noticed the two books he laid down on the table before pulling out his chair and wondered if he was also researching past ancestors.

On the wall facing Tessa a large clock chimed in its low base sound to the count of three. The young man waited as the third note sounded, then self consciously nodded. He sat, then stood again suddenly and offered his hand across the table. "Wes Shepherd."

"Tessa O'Neil," Tessa answered and quickly shook his hand in greeting.

Tessa noticed him reading the titles of the books she had chosen from the library shelves. "Are you just starting out?" he asked, nodding at the yet unopened books.

"I suppose you'd say so. I'm looking for a family that doesn't seem to exist before the 1891 census."

He appeared genuinely interested and swept his hair back from his eyes as he readjusted his chair. He had dark hair, darker than Tessa's; almost black, that matched the thin moustache hugging his upper lip. His face was sun-tanned and had an olive complexion. His dark eyes smiled at her from across the table. "Well, there are many reasons why that may be, although the '81 census records are usually pretty good." He reached across and picked up the top most book.

"So, I take it your people are rich and are from Devon England."

"You take it correctly." Tessa said, "though, they're not my people. I'm treating it as missing persons case for a client who hired my firm to look into her family."

"What about yourself?" Tessa nodded toward the two books laying next to his laptop, both of which offered help in deciphering Latin records.

"I'm back to the 1600s and many entries are in Latin; that's the Yorkshire branch. The other side is Scots-Irish. I'm

16

only back to 1830 on that side. My Grandfather often referred to us as Black Irish and said his grandfather could remember the woman in our family who danced Spanish dances." He noticed Tessa's expression and realized she had never heard that term before. "Oh ... Black Irish is an old term referring to Irish who have darker features supposedly inherited from shipwrecked Spaniards from the wrecked Armada. Many found themselves on Irish soil and stayed. At least that's what I grew up being told, there's not a lot of literature about it. But it has always intrigued me ... so I'm looking."

He laughed softly. "Sometimes I'm sorry I even started this search. It seems to take up most of my free time. But you, being an investigator should realize the thrill of the hunt. After all, these people existed or else we wouldn't be here."

She nodded in agreement. "How long have you been looking?"

"Only a couple of years. I started this because I wanted to write a book about our family. You know—something to give all the relatives at Christmas. But now after researching for a while I thought perhaps a book about my genealogical journey instead; advice on how to start, something that might help others. It's not easy researching British ancestors from Canada."

"I'm just thankful there are a lot of records on line to help me start looking."

"True, but be careful never to assume anything. Just because you find a person with the name you're seeking at the right location and time doesn't mean it's the right person. It's a good place to start but things must be verified. When I started, I got taken down the wrong road by following a cousin with the same name. That's common because families often stuck to firm rules about naming children." When he noticed Tessa wasn't following, he explained further. "The first son was usually named after the father's father. The second son was named after the mother's father, the third son was named after the father. The same applied for daughters but the reverse, the first daughter was named after the mother's mother etc. So, if you had two sons and they each had a son, they –if the rule was followed—could have the same first name. Not always mind you but it did happen in my case and I followed the wrong one. He was in the right place at the right time and I just assumed he was the correct person." Another thought occurred to him. "Also, if a child died, they would often reuse the name. So, you have to be careful."

He looked up as an elderly woman passed by their table led by the library volunteer who was eagerly making research suggestions. He smiled at Tessa as he passed, pleased she seemed to have taken his advice.

"You mentioned that the family doesn't seem to exist before 1891. What have you found so far?" He opened his laptop, as if preparing to make some rough notes.

"Well, I have his full name, place of birth and birth date, according to his granddaughter. I have his second marriage, an 1881 civil registration record and his daughter's birth registration the following year. I know his sons were Jo and Wil and their approximate ages and I know roughly when and where they died."

"That's a lot more than some people have when they start to search," he said, smiling at her enthusiasm.

Tessa opened her note pad and produced the two civil registration records she had printed. "I've checked all England for the father and the sons, but I can't find the family. I even tried the 1871 and 1861 census records and no Cyrus Griffin."

"There are many reasons for not finding a family. Their name could be misspelled or misinterpreted in the online indexing by someone who couldn't make out the name in the original records. That often happens, for example Williamson is often misread as Wilkinson. They could have left the country temporarily, they might be living with another family who gave the wrong information, maybe the family name changed, or the records could be simply unreadable."

"And I thought this was going to be easy."

"Sometimes you get lucky and it is, but not often." He smiled in reference to his own work.

The quiet clock chimed its half hour ring. "Oh," she said, and instinctively checked her watch and verified the time. "I'm sorry. I'll have to rush off. I have an appointment at four o'clock."

He rose as she stood and gathered up her belongings. "Perhaps we'll meet again. I'll be here again tomorrow. If you need some direction, I would be pleased to help."

Tessa appreciated the offer, then smiled. "Thank you, I may just take you up on that. Good bye."

At the book checkout desk, she casually glanced back. Wes was typing on his laptop and seemed absorbed in his research books.

She would have preferred to stay at the library and talk about her work with this new friend, but as it was, she was scheduled to meet with Hannah Wentworth at four o'clock and didn't want to be late.

Chapter 3

She climbed the five steps to the front door of Hannah's two-storey home a little before her appointment time. She was greeted by Duffy, the same butler she had met the previous day and he smiled at her as he opened the door and indicated his mistress was waiting for her in the small library. His hair was silver grey, and he appeared to be in his late seventies. He had a clipped London accent and Tessa supposed Hannah had brought her butler with her when she left England some twenty-five years ago. Now she was living in Toronto most of the year and spent the warmer months in her summer home in Niagara-on-the-Lake.

Duffy seemed glad to see Tessa again and escorted her to the library as a young man with a disgruntled look was leaving. He gave her a dismissive nod as he passed by, obviously upset about something. The elderly woman was waiting for her and greeted her with a warm smile.

Hannah sat in her favourite wing chair, the velvet fabric matching her light, blue eyes. She had sent her maid for tea and as the tray was being placed on a table before them, dismissed her footman who closed the door and left them in private as the maid prepared the tea.

She was glad to see Tessa again and brightened with the opportunity to discuss her family.

"After you left, I remembered that I had a box with some of my grandfather's papers. Perhaps they might be of help." She smiled. "I suppose you met Kevin; he was leaving as you arrived."

Tessa smiled back at her. "You mean the young man with the scowl."

"Well, he's not so enthusiastic about my hiring a detective. He thinks he can find the information himself. His father had been my attorney for over twenty years, and he thinks he knows what's best for me. I guess he feels a bit protective."

"I suppose that's part of his job, but don't worry, I will find out about your Uncle Jeremy and I will have the documents to prove any of his descendants are related to you grandfather." She set her tea cup down then took Hannah's cup from her as well.

"I asked for you, you know," she said, matter-of-factly, "after I saw an article about you finding that adopted little girl. That's why I called your firm—I know you will find him."

This surprised Tessa. So, it wasn't a grunt job after all, given to her because she was the most junior member of the team.

"Have you begun the search yet?" Hannah asked, her voice hopeful.

"Yes, but I can't seem to find them on the 1881 census yet. I was hoping you might have something that would help. You mentioned some of your grandfather's papers. Perhaps they might assist me in locating the family."

"Yes. You may go Agatha." This last was said to the maid who stood patiently by the door waiting in case she was needed. Hannah waited until the library door had closed. "There is a small black box on the book shelf ... if you wouldn't mind." She waved her hand toward a large piece of furniture that hugged the wall on one side of the room. Tessa noticed the small box sitting among many photographs, books, and figurines and went to retrieve the wooden box.

"Thank you." Hannah opened the lid reverently then pulled out the only two pieces of paper in the box. "That's strange. I thought there were more documents." She unfolded the first and announced that this was the certificate of her grandfather's second marriage to Emily. She smiled thinking of her grandmother. "This might be of some help," she said, offering the document to Tessa. "I was certain there were other documents ... but they don't seem to be here now." She looked puzzled, as if perhaps she had misplaced something, something she was certain had been there, and was trying to remember. She moved the last paper aside slowly as if wishing would make the others appear. The second paper proved to be a birth certificate for her mother, Isabel. "I'm not sure now ..." Hannah said, distressed at not finding the documents she had promised and as Tessa watched she could see the mental reality hit Hannah that perhaps she had only imagined more documents.

Her face brightened as she drew out the first of two necklaces that had been kept safely stored in the box.

"This was the first gift my grandfather gave to my grandmother." Holding up the spectacular emerald necklace she continued, "He gave this to his new bride on the day of their wedding." She drew out the second piece of jewellery. "My grandmother loved him so much that she had this locket made on their first anniversary. She had taken a small clip of his hair and had it encased in the back of the locket, so he would always be with her ... touching her."

"That's very romantic," Tessa said softly. Hannah handed her the locket to look at. It was the usual size for a locket and opened to reveal a place for the pictures of the happy couple, but instead of flowers or similar romantic themes etching the round cover; it was decorated with the mythical—part lion and part eagle—griffin on the front. "It's very beautiful."

"She loved him very much and when he died, she was devastated. She died three months later ... of a broken heart my mother said." She gently placed the necklace and locket back in their felt lined box. Tessa returned the small box to its resting place on the shelf.

For the rest of her visit Hannah reminisced about her family and talked about her quiet life now that travelling had become more difficult for her. It was five-thirty when Tessa left, determined more than ever to help Hannah find her lost family.

She hadn't had much sleep. Thoughts of Hannah Wentworth's request had kept her mind busy and unable to rest. Why should a family that had shown up so prominently on three census records, now disappear? She had tried to find Cyrus Griffin's birth record with no results. She had attempted to find the father's family using the name Cyrus had given on his second marriage certificate, but nothing. There didn't appear to be a merchant in Exeter named Geoffrey Griffin.

It was three in the morning before she had finally fallen asleep and now after a late rising; a quick breakfast while she checked in with her firm regarding her progress; Tessa now found herself back at the local library.

For modern searches she had no problem. She had her connections and knew how to find out about people in this electronic world. Many genealogical sites had lists of professional researchers who—for a fee—would search the records at hand. That might be an option down the road but that might also take longer than she wanted.

The elevator door opened, and Tessa again found herself on the top floor in the genealogical section of the library. The older volunteer who had helped her last day had been replaced today by another volunteer. A young woman this time, who sat at the same desk texting on her phone.

The long table from yesterday had two younger men seated together at the one end. They were quietly discussing something they had found on a library computer and stopped momentarily as Tessa passed them. There were some books at the other end of the table across from where she had sat yesterday, and she recognized the titles of the books as the ones Wes had chosen to help him with Latin translations. She wondered if he had changed his mind and left them there after she had gone to her meeting. She glanced around. Other than the two men, she seemed to be the only other patron on the floor. Tessa sat her bag on the table and pulled out her laptop. She doubted the young woman was as enthused about family history as the older man she met yesterday so thought better than asking any complicated questions. If she was honest with herself, she was hoping Wes would be here to offer some guidance.

Just then he appeared from behind a book shelf, his laptop carried open with its cord dangling. He smiled when he saw Tessa. "Well, hello again." He saw her glance at the cord as it hit his chair. "I've been sitting on the floor for the last twenty minutes charging this beast." He set the machine down carefully as he unplugged the cord. He looked satisfied with the results. "I'm good for a couple of hours now."

"How did you make out with your searching?"

"Not too well, I'm afraid. I tried variations of the name or potential misspellings. I've tried just searching for someone named Cyrus and leaving the last name blank. I looked for his sons and his father ... nothing."

Wes moved his books aside as he sat down, then re-positioned his laptop. He brought up the page he had made notes on yesterday. "Well, don't forget not every family history site has all the information. Most are constantly adding new material and updating. Which are you using?"

"I thought I'd start with Ancestry and see what I might find."

"That's a good place to start especially if you're researching Britain. I like the Family Search site and Find My Past, but there are dozens of others: The Genealogist, London Lives, London Metropolitan Archives, the National Archives at Kew are a few, and of course all the Family History Societies."

Family Search is the Mormon site. There is a church in town—The Church of The Latter-Day Saints."

Tessa took some notes so as not to forget.

"You can go and search for the record you need then order the film with the actual document. Sometimes the documents aren't available on line yet, but the church will usually have them." He smiled as she quickened her writing. "There is also another free site called-Free BMD." He noticed her questioned look. "Births, marriages and deaths for Britain. Then there's newspapers of the day, school admission records, court records, military records, and I'm sure much more that I'm not aware of."

"I'm glad you were here today; I was beginning to think this was something I couldn't do. Normally I'd have my police sources, the media, my informants, but this ..." She gave her hand a dismissive wave.

"It's always a bit overwhelming at first, but the good thing is, you know they did exist. It's just a matter of finding them." He pushed his laptop across the table, so Tessa could see the screen. Then tucking his chair in he came around and pulled out a chair beside Tessa and sat next to her, so they could both see the screen. "So, let's go over what you have so far." Tessa showed him the records she had discovered so far. Wes began to make a chart with names and dates, based upon the census records from 1891 to 1911.

The chart listed a few facts and was much easier to read than the notes she had taken. "Okay, we have Cyrus Thomas Griffin and if he didn't lie on his marriage certificate, we know his father's name was Geoffrey Griffin, a tea merchant."

"You mean people would lie when filling out an official document?"

Wes laughed, then spoke softly after the volunteer flashed him a censorious look. "Yes, all the time. People lied about their age mostly. Often the father's occupation would be socially elevated just to make the bridegroom appear more important than he was."

He started typing. "We know his sons were Joe, Will and Jeremy." Tessa watched as he added the names of the three boys.

"No," she said. "The spelling is different." She opened her notebook and checked the information she had been given. "It's Jo and Wil."

He leaned a bit closer as she found the page. She could smell his cologne and was distracted for a moment. "That's curious. Why would you spell the boys names that way?"

Tessa had thought the same thing when Hannah had given her further information about her family.

"Well, if Jo is short for Joseph, I can see that, but spelling Wil with one 'l' is strange in that William has two, so why not spell it that way." Tessa checked her notes, also the 1891 census and her spellings were correct.

The large clock chimed one o'clock in its low drone. "That reminds me," he whispered, as the librarian volunteer walked by. "I'm starting to get hungry. Care to join me for lunch? There's a nice place around the corner ... my treat." "Thank you, yes. I'd like that."

Cyrus Thomas Griffin's Families

31

Chapter 4

They sat in a booth near the window facing each other and Tessa was suddenly aware of him. He was much taller than her five feet, eight inches, straight of body, with wide shoulders. He hadn't shaved that morning which gave him a rugged, outdoors look. His dark hair was swept back by the sunglasses he placed on his head and his brown eyes smiled at her. "I'm glad you came back to the library," he said, then lowered his voice as the waitress handed them their menus. She noticed his hands as they held the black folder with the days specials slipped through the plastic on the front cover.

"I thought the same thing about you," she said. "To be honest I was beginning to realize how little I knew about genealogy, and when I got stopped at 1881, I wasn't sure where to look or how."

He glanced aside as the waitress returned for their order, then left them to their conversation.

"Is Wes short for Wesley?"

He smiled. "My father would like to think so. He wanted me named after his grandfather, Wesley Shepherd but my mother didn't think the name Wesley sounded authoritative enough for a lawyer, so she changed it to Weston. Her father was a lawyer," he added with a shrug. "So, as long as my name is shortened to Wes, Mum and Dad are both happy."

"So, what do you do for a living?"

"I'm a criminal lawyer."

Her eyes widened. "Really?"

"No." He smiled at the look on her face. "I'm a teacher. I've taken a year's leave before moving to China."

Tessa waited until the waitress set down her salmon and salad then placed burger and fries in front of Wes.

He picked up a french fry and dipped it in the ketchup he had squirted on his plate. "I don't believe it!" He lay it down again visibly upset with something.

"What? What is it?"

"I just broke the most important rule of genealogy: never assume anything!"

Tessa put her tea cup down and waited as Wes explained further. His face brightened as he suddenly couldn't wait to share this epiphany. "You had it all along, with my name. You assumed it was short for Wesley." She gave him an encouraging look not quite sure what he was getting at.

"Don't you see? Jo might not mean Joseph and Wil might be something other than William. That might be why you couldn't find them."

He picked up his burger, pleased with his deduction and took a big bite, then swept his plate aside making room for his laptop that he had brought with them. Tessa followed suit and took her notebook from her bag.

Wes opened-up a window with the page he had started earlier. "You found the family in 1891 but we don't know where they were for the ten years between 1881 and 1891.

"Somewhere in there the boys went to school. Do you have the birth dates for the two oldest boys?" She flipped through her research pages as he typed a note about the names.

"Okay, so when he was married again in 1882 the boys would be around six and four and this shows he was living in the London area. Where did they live in 1891?"

Tessa pulled out the folded census record from 1891 and handed it to Wes.

"So now the boys would be about fifteen and thirteen. Somewhere during this time, the boys probably went to a private school. From the second marriage certificate we know they lived in Islington, at least during the time of their wedding so let's look for the boys on some school records, maybe we might find out something new."

It sounded like a plan and maybe there were also other records. "What about Jo's army records?" she suggested. "We can check out his attestation form and see if his name is Joseph or something else."

"Very good. You're better at this than you think. We can also check deaths of British citizens overseas."

"We?"

"Yes, if you'll allow me. I'd like to help you." He reached over and took another bite of his burger, wiping his hands on the napkin before typing on his laptop. "Besides, I was getting bored with my search. Maybe if I take a break and tackle it later, I might see something I've missed. Your people sound a lot more interesting."

"I would like that. Thank you." They finished their lunch in companionable silence and before leaving to return home Wes had given her the sites he used and his passwords, so she could try those as well as the one she was using.

Tessa sat down at her coffee table, her laptop open and with the screen ready to search. She placed her bowl of mac and cheese to the side—a hurried supper—her tabby cat nestled in a blanket placed at the end of the sofa.

"Okay, Tabs, let's see what we can find tonight." The cat gave her an approving yawn then went back to sleep with its paws covering its face.

She went into Ancestry and tried using the wild card symbol so, she typed in Jo* Griffin. The results came back quickly indicating that there were too many matches to display. She tried again with Jos*. The first twelve pages of results were of a variety of Joseph Griffins in Britain, so she went further hoping to find some different variations. After twenty-three pages she stopped and decided to take a different path.

"Let's ask Google for boy names that begin with the letters Jo." She pressed enter and after a moment reading the various sites that came up, she chose the first one and was rewarded with a full-page list of names. "Now, let's narrow this to names that sound like Joe if they were shortened." She ruled out Jonathan, Joshua, and Jordan for now. There were three, that caught her eye; Jonah, Joel and Josiah. She wasn't sure if Joel was a nineteenth-century name or not but wrote all down as possibilities.

She smiled at the sleeping cat who had now rolled over, his tummy slowing rising and lowering as it slept, and scooped up another forkful of the creamy pasta. "Now we're getting somewhere." She went to the Ancestry site and typed in all the necessary information—Josiah Griffin, born 1876 give or take five years, in Devon, then pressed enter. There were pages of

Josiah Griffins. But as she scrolled down each page, none of the Josiah Griffins listed were of the right age or from the right area. Many had been census records that didn't apply, being either too early or too late. Tessa patiently checked each page before proceeding to the next. There were two that she found in Devon on the 1881 census, and although the age didn't match, she checked them anyway just in case a mistake in transcribing had happened.

There were two other sites Wes had suggested, so opening-up another window she typed in 'Find My Past' and waited for the site to come up. She logged in with the password Wes had provided to her and decided to check out deaths in India.

Tessa typed in the name, Jo, leaving off the last letters and then entered the dates for birth and death. Next, she typed in the word 'India' for location, then pressed enter. Over three hundred results came up, so she narrowed the search to just military results and discovered three names. Two Josiah references for marriages and one Josias, for a death. She opened the death record and found this Josias had died in northern India after being wounded during a tribal conflict. She finished up her mac and cheese while staring at the record. This looked like it could be Hannah's uncle. She felt her heart race at the thought and had to share her excitement. But she wanted to be sure first. There must be a record of his enlistment somewhere.

Next Tessa went to the British National Archives site. If Josias had been a career soldier it made sense that he would have been in the first World War. She found the Army and Militia section then went to the British Army WWI service Records 1914-1920.

The screen took her back to Ancestry which she guessed was somehow affiliated with the archives. Then she saw it. Under, name and address of next of kin was the name she was hoping to see; Cyrus Griffin, Piccadilly Road London, relationship—father. "We found it!" Startled, the tabby cat left the warm bed on the sofa and wandered off into the kitchen his ears back, disgruntled at having been woken.

Tessa gathered her notebook and found the phone number Wes had given her. "Wes? I found him!"

"Wonderful! Have you confirmed it?"

"Yes, I found his attestation form with his father's name on it."

"Great work, now we just have to find him on the '81 census."

"First try looking in the '81 census with the name you

have then if that doesn't work, plug in just the first name and leave the surname blank. It might take a long time but hopefully you will find the right one." There was a pause, then he added, "Shall we meet tomorrow at the diner and compare notes?"

"Thanks, I can be there at noon."

Chapter 5

The sun shone early, a welcome change from the last two days of chilly wind and drizzle. Tessa sat at her kitchen table; the front page of the morning newspaper opened to its full length before her.

Hannah Wentworth was dead. Her passing in the night had been peaceful and age related, said the papers. There would be no funeral or memorial, at her request. After all she had no family and most of her friends who hadn't preceded her were in no condition to attend such a gathering. Tessa read the death notice over again and was saddened at the thought. Hannah seemed so happy and well yesterday. She wished she could have reassured Hannah that she did indeed have family. But that wasn't the main concern of the news article. Who would get her millions? That was the real story they cared about, and Tessa was sure that all the world asked the same question. Tabby walked across the paper rubbing his head along her arm as Tessa read further.

The phone rang, and she wondered who would be calling so early. "Yes, right away."
Her office had called, asking her to come in earlier than she had planned. Hannah's lawyer probably wanted an update to

help with any possible inheritance. It was an hour later, and Tessa was waiting for her boss to arrive. He'd been to an executive meeting and was expected any moment.

"I've just spoken to Kevin Fairchild. He won't be requiring our services any longer."

"But, I've almost found Hannah's family," Tessa protested.

"He assures me that he has found a credible heir of Cyrus Griffin based on records he's found in Hannah's personal files. So that's that. Hanley has a new case for you to start on." He picked up a folder from the desk. "A Mary Rockford who's trying to locate her birth parents." He smiled broadly. "Right up your alley."

Something wasn't right. Tessa remembered Kevin Fairchild, the sour young man whom she had seen at Hannah's home and wondered how he would have found out something that she herself hadn't found yet. She wondered about the papers Hannah had thought she had lost, the certificates that she had thought were in the small box. "Couldn't I just have another few days ... just to confirm what he has found?"

〜

He shook his head slowly. "He's paid us in full and the case is closed." After all, he thought, Kevin had assured him he had all the necessary documents from Hannah's safe deposit box and had the proof he required for the courts; a young man named Edmond Nolan was a direct, and only heir to Hannah's millions—him being a newly discovered great-grandson of Cyrus Griffin.

Tessa nodded slowly. "I understand," she said. "I'll check with Hanley about the new case." She'd been dismissed and was saddened she hadn't found Hannah's family first. She wondered how long Hannah's lawyer had known about Cyrus's great-grandson yet hadn't told Hannah. Why had he been so upset at Hannah hiring her? If he knew all along Hannah had family, wouldn't he want to corroborate the find? Something didn't seem right about all of this.

Wes waved to her from the back of the crowded diner at the same booth they had sat in a day earlier. He rose as she removed her coat, helping to hold her laptop bag as she sat down.

"I found them!" he said, excitement barely contained on his face. "It took most of the night, but I found them in Devonport, Devon."

She felt his enthusiasm, "How?"

The waitress came over and offered them menus. They ordered tea; Tessa, being too upset to eat and Wes, too tired. "I went through every 1881 census record I could find with a child named Josiah or Josias, leaving the last name blank. I found the family around four in the morning living ... on a street I think, or area, called Knackers Knowle. He smiled then pulled out a paper that he had printed for Tessa and handed it to her triumphantly. "So much for the traditional baby names." He smiled as she took the paper.

Tessa opened the folded paper slowly, then scanned the names for the one they knew for sure was Cyrus Griffin's son. Mid-page was the name Alexander Fenwick with his sons, Josias Fenwick, Wilson Fenwick, and the youngest, three-month old Jeremy Fenwick, only the baby was listed as a female.

She gave Wes a questioning look. "Obviously the information was written incorrectly by the enumerator. There was no wife mentioned so I checked the records for a death and found a Mary Ann Fenwick who died a month after the baby was born. There's a fifth name listed in the household a James Tyrell described as border." He showed her how to tell which households belonged together by the enumerator's double slash marks. "It seems Cyrus changed his name

43

sometime after 1881, which is rather unusual." Wes sensed something was wrong by Tessa's quiet demeanour. "What's wrong? I thought you'd be pleased?"

"I love that you found them but it's all pretty much academic now."

The waitress returned with their tea and Wes waited for her to leave before questioning Tessa. "Why? What happened?"

"Hannah Wentworth died last night. I feel bad about it. She was so happy yesterday, hopeful that I could find her uncle's family." Tessa added sugar and milk to her tea, then shrugged. "Now my assignment's been cancelled by Hannah's lawyer. He told my boss he's found an heir already—an Edmond Nolan, apparently a great-grandson of Cyrus Griffin."

"That seems strange."

"I know. A lot doesn't make sense unless he knew all along. Maybe he has documents that show who Cyrus Griffin really was."

"So, what will you do now?"

"I'm not sure yet. I have another case I have to work on, but I have a month for that, so I'll take a week off before I tackle it." She shook her head slowly and looked at Wes. "My gut is telling me; something is not right about this. Why didn't the lawyer tell Hannah about a living relative? Why suddenly stop my investigation? You'd think he would be pleased to get the results of my search."

"Maybe he has more invested than you know. Who gets her money if there is no relative?"

"She told me most of it would go to charities after she took care of her household staff."

Tessa took a slow sip of her tea, her mind racing. "I've got a week to look into this on my own time. Thanks to you I have a place to start and if I find an Edmond Nolan then all well and good. If there are others, then the court should be informed." She smiled at Wes, pleased with her decision.

Wes nodded in agreement. "Look, I'm going north tomorrow to visit my grandmother. Why don't you come along? She has Wi-Fi up there and we could work faster on this together."

This was a something she hadn't expected. The sincere look in his eyes made her contemplate the idea.

"Well, I suppose it doesn't matter where I work,"—she gave him a conspiratorial look— "and I would appreciate your help. But that wouldn't be fair to you and your grandmother, you've done so much for me already. I probably would never have found the family on my own."

"Nonsense, of course you would have," he said, "... eventually. Besides, Nan would like someone other than me to cook for, I'm sure."

"I'd have to take Tabby over to my sister's house. What time are you planning to leave?"

"I usually leave around five in the morning, so I can beat the Toronto traffic, but we can go whenever you're ready."

She had only known this man a few days, she liked him and trusted him and besides she needed time to think and a few days up north might just help her see things clearer, yet for some reason the thought crossed her mind, that this all seemed too pat, too coincidental. She put that thought aside. "I can be ready by five." She quickly wrote down her address and phone number. "Here, I'll see you tomorrow. I want to go to Hannah's house and talk to Duffy before we go. Maybe he can tell me something more about this lawyer of Hannah's." She gathered her belongings and put on her jacket. "Thank you, Wes, I'm looking forward to working together."

He smiled warmly at her. "Me too. See you tomorrow."

It was two o'clock before Tessa drove up to Hannah Wentworth's Niagara-on-the-Lake home. She wasn't sure what she would find or say when she knocked on the door, but she

46

hadn't expected to find a grieving Duffy, his eyes red-rimmed and tired-looking as he showed her in. "Good afternoon, Miss Tessa."

"I was so sorry to hear about Hannah," she said, as she was escorted into the hallway. "I wish I could have helped her find her family before ..."

"I'm glad you have come by," Duffy said, as he indicated they move into the library. The drapes had been drawn back revealing the room as she had first seen it only this time the desk was empty of papers and books and Hannah was not at her favourite place in the pale blue chair. Once inside, Duffy picked up the small black box that sat on the side board. The same box that Hannah had asked her to retrieve from the book shelf. "After you left, Miss Hannah asked me to make sure you were given this box. She liked you. I think she knew her time was soon over." His eyes glistened from the emotion he was feeling. "You know, I've been with her for over forty years. She was like my family. I will miss her greatly."

Tessa took the proffered box reverently. She paused before opening it. "This was very kind of her." She unhooked the hasp. "I liked her too." Inside was the gold locket. She fingered the etching on the cover—a griffin, a symbol of Hannah's family; then placed it gently back in its felt resting

47

place. "Thank you, I will treasure it."

"What will you do now?" she asked, wondering if he would go back to London.

"Stay here, probably. Miss Hannah has been very generous. She has seen to all her staff. This house,"—he waved his arm to encompass the room they were in— "has been left to me and I shall continue to care for it." He turned toward the vast wall of windows, facing Lake Ontario. Old Fort Niagara could be seen at the entrance to the Niagara River. "She liked to sit in this room and look out at the ships on the lake." Tessa looked out at the calm blue expanse of Lake Ontario, empty today of shipping travel. "Her ashes will be scattered on the lake." he said, quietly.

Tessa ventured as to her reason for coming. She had established a rapport with the aging butler and hoped he might be able to answer some of her questions. "I'm going to continue investigating even though our firm has been dismissed. Apparently, her lawyer has found an heir on his own." This latter had the effect she had hoped for. "Do you know of any papers or certificates that Hannah may have had regarding her grandfather?"

Duffy looked troubled by this. "There were papers. I know Miss Hannah was worried she had lost them, but I also know Mr. Fairchild has many documents, some he acquired from his father while he was looking after Miss Hannah's finances and some he got later after Miss Hannah showed him what she had found among her grandfather's things. I don't know whether she gave them to him or if he took them for safe keeping." He shook his head sadly. "She was beginning to forget things; I suppose it was for her protection."

Chapter 6

It was quiet for the first half hour, both outside and inside the vehicle. After taking Tabby to her sister's home and a bit of necessary shopping, she had had only a short hour or so of sleep. Her mind kept thinking, leaving her restless and tired. Tessa had woken around three-thirty then hurriedly gathered enough clothing and toiletries for a week's stay, but once comfortable in Wes's SUV, had dozed off after they had merged onto the highway.

Wes showed up earlier than planned. He had confessed after, that he would have been content to park outside her home until signs of life appeared but as it was, Tessa was packed and ready— although not quite awake—her bags and research materials at the front door.

Tessa was glad Keefer had called her on her home phone rather than on her cell phone during her trip.

"Your hunch was right," he started. "He's not a teacher."

"What then?"

"He works for a company called Anderson and Wiley. They're a security and investigative company providing protection for people and goods."

Keefer waited for Tessa to comment on his findings but when she didn't, he added, "Looks like that lawyer fellow is taking no chance of you finding out anything to contradict his lost heir. Seems he's hired someone to keep an eye on you."

She had explained the situation to her long-time investigator friend and now with his report had second thoughts about who Weston Shepherd really was and his motives in asking her up to his grandmother's place. "Yeah, it looks that way. Thanks for this. I'll keep you informed while I'm gone. Don't call or text me just in case, I'll contact you if I need anything."

A transport truck sped past them breaking the quiet the early morning had promised; the noise jolting Tessa into wakefulness.

"Good morning." Wes smiled at her as she yawned discreetly, then focused again on the road ahead.

"Sorry, I didn't mean to fall asleep. I just couldn't keep my eyes open." She looked out toward the lake, dark and calm with a sparkle of lights on the far shore. The traffic was picking up now, a few transport trucks but mostly cars on their daily commute. "How long do you think it will take to get to your grandmother's?"

"Maybe five hours, but that's with a stop along the way. Her place is on a lake just south of Algonquin Park."

Traffic picked up once they got to the Burlington Skyway, a large bridge spanning the west end of Lake Ontario. The first signs of dawn appeared over the lake and within minutes the sun was shining into her passenger window.

"You didn't get much sleep last night?"

"No, I kept thinking about Hannah. I liked her. I wish I could have found out about any possible relatives for her. Then I thought about her grandfather. How could he leave a child behind?"

"Well let's cut him some slack. Life wasn't easy in the 1880s. Maybe he had no choice. He had no wife. He couldn't look after an infant himself. Maybe he was offered work in London." He paused as he passed a slower vehicle ahead of them. "I'm sure we'll figure it out."

"I hope so, one way or another I want to finish this job."

Once on Highway 401 East, the early morning sun shone low in the sky directly in front of them. Tessa lowered her visor to help with the sudden glare.

He noticed her staring at the dash as if lost in thought.

"You're awfully quiet."

"Just thinking."

"About Hannah?" Wes passed a slower moving truck then pulled back into the right lane.

"Yeah. I was beginning to feel a connection with her. It never occurred to me she would die later, so sudden."

"Sad as it is, she was ninety-eight. It was bound to happen eventually." He put on his sunglasses which had been resting on the rear-view mirror support.

"I know, I just have the feeling that something's wrong. I don't trust her lawyer and as soon as I find the truth—no matter what it is—I'll feel better."

Wes reached back behind her seat and pulled out a pillow he had brought along. "Here, you might as well catch up on some sleep. No need for both of us to stay awake."

"Thanks." She adjusted her seat belt and made herself comfortable.

A quick braking motion jarred her awake with Wes's arm outstretched across her. "Sorry, didn't mean to wake you, that car just cut me off." He motioned to the small red Volkswagen ahead of them that suddenly picked up speed then swerved to the outer lane cutting off another car in the same way.

Tessa checked the dash clock and realized she had been sleeping for the last two hours.

"Where are we?"

"Just past Haliburton. Not long now."

You could smell the difference in the air: the scent of pine. "You know, I've never been this far north before."

"Really? You've never been camping or fishing with your family?"

She smiled thinking of the short trips her family made to local camps. "A few times but to places around Niagara. Once we went to Shangri-La Valley ... just for the one night. We had a camp fire." She smiled thinking about it. "You know, I haven't thought about that in years. I don't even remember if we stayed the night in a tent or just came home when it got late."

"Then you have a pleasant surprise waiting for you."

He signalled, then slowed down to approach a wayside diner. "Time for a break."

The diner staff seemed to recognize Wes. He waved a hello to the man behind the grill and walked to a booth nearest the window. It was a long narrow diner and from the outside seemed like a mobile home someone had converted into a one-room eatery. There were booths lined along the front below large windows. Individual seating ran along the counter top that went the length of the diner. It seemed to be both a popular truck-stop and local hangout. An eighteen-wheeler pulled into the large parking space at the side of the diner. Tessa watched as two men left their cab, entered, and joined three other men at the counter. There was sudden laughter as the diner owner shared a story with the new comers.

"This seems a popular place."

"Mainly in the summer. Joe and his wife have built up a reputation for good food and a clean establishment." He accepted the menus the waitress handed him and passed one to Tessa. "Once the truckers start coming, word gets around pretty quickly. They have a liquor licence too, so that helps keep the locals coming."

Wes ordered the breakfast special for them both and sipped on the coffee that had arrived with their menus. Tessa watched as he drank, wondering about this man. How was he going to stop her searching for the truth? Would he lead her to a fake family and ultimately a dead end? She felt a bit guilty at questioning his kindness, yet she would be mindful of what Keefer had told her and remain vigilant.

He smiled when he noticed her watching him. "What

are you thinking?"

"About us working together on this. I can't thank you enough for offering. It's not really my job anymore but I still feel as if I owe Hannah the truth." She took a sip of her coffee as their meal arrived. "It sounds silly, but I feel she's watching us and is happy we are doing this for her." She smiled at the thought.

"All we can do is our best."

It was after nine when they turned off the main road onto a compacted gravel lane-way that led to the cottage. "It's about another fifteen minutes," Wes had said as they signalled their turn.

"I remember one hill here that my father took a little too fast. He was towing the boat behind us at the time. When he hit the top of the hill there was a depression across the road and the trailer bounced as it crossed it. Next thing we knew the boat was sitting on the trailer sideways." He laughed at the memory. "It was my father's first boat and I guess he didn't have it secured tightly enough to the trailer. Never happened again though. We used to hold our breath in anticipation whenever we came up, hoping for another hilarious incident." He paused, remembering. "We used to tease Dad a lot about that."

"Where are your parents now" She asked, hoping it wasn't too personal a question.

"They moved to Portugal after dad retired. They spend the winter there then come back to New York State for the summer. They have a place in the Finger Lakes region. I think Nan misses their visits, but my brother Tony and I come up when we can, to help. Nan refuses to give up her home so there's a lot to be done that she can't do on her own."

The cottage looked a lot like a one-story bungalow to Tessa, but then again, she wasn't sure what to expect aside from a log cabin type of structure. Wes's grandmother had heard them arrive and was at the back door ready to greet them. She waved as Wes parked in a small space at the back of the cottage.

Lilian Shepherd was a tall woman with colouring that didn't differ greatly from her grandson's 'Black Irish" looks. Wes greeted her with a hug and kiss then introduced his guest. "You made good time." She said, then looked at Tessa and smiled. "You must be tired, dear." Lilian Shepherd made her welcome and showed her to the one of three bedrooms next to the bathroom that lined the back of the cottage. The front half of the cottage overlooking the lake contained the large kitchen and adjoining living room with stone fireplace and enormous picture window.

After freshening up Tessa joined Wes at the kitchen counter for coffee and biscuits.

"Tessa is interested in genealogy too and has come up to work on a project with me," Wes explained. There was a corner at the far end of the living room that had been set up as a small office area with desk and computer.

"Sounds like a working vacation."

"Some what, but I'll work on what needs to be done on the cottage before we go.

While Wes rested, his grandmother entertained Tessa with stories of cottage life. They sat on the front deck while listening to the sounds of the lake water as it lapped rhythmically against the dock.

"Do you like living here?" Tessa asked, wondering how an elderly woman managed all the work that a home needed, on her own.

Nan smiled. She seemed younger than her seventy-six years, her hair still the dark brown it was in her younger days as she refused to let the grey show by colouring it. Tessa thought she must have been a stunning girl with the bright blue eyes standing out amid the dark complexion. She could see Wes in her features. Tessa could hear her Irish heritage in the odd word she spoke.

"I've always enjoyed the north. That's what drew me to my husband. He loved nature. And when he found this place, I agreed to live here."

"It must be difficult at times, especially in winter."

She smiled at the thought. "There aren't a lot of people up here then, that's true. But I've never been one to feel lonely. I enjoy my own company. I have my books, and my hobbies to keep me occupied. Sometimes my son and his wife visit, just to check on me I guess, with the excuse of bringing up some groceries. Then there's the boys, Tony and Wes come up and make sure everything is in working order."

"I suppose you will miss him when he goes to teach in China," Tessa suggested hoping to get a confirmation, hoping Keefer had been misinformed.

A moment of doubt crossed Nan's face, then faded just as quickly easing her features. "It will be a great opportunity for Wes." A wind gust blew a few leaves along the length of the deck, then she swept her hair back.

"You're the first woman he's brought up here to meet me," she said quietly, hoping Tessa would elaborate on the relationship.

Tessa understood her interest, after all Wes was an important member of her family and eldest grandson. "We're just friends. In fact, we just met two days ago at the library." That seemed rather vague, even to her. "He's offered to help me with some important research I'm involved in." Then she added, "I'm most grateful for his expertise."

Chapter 7

As Nan attended to their culinary needs Tessa and Wes worked on their search during the early part of the afternoon. Tessa watched the tiny humming birds that visited the feeder that hung just outside the main window as Wes located the information page on his laptop, readying to begin. She noticed how the birds would chase each other away from the feeder into the nearby pines, allowing others to quickly take their place at the sweet nectar, then repeat the process as others took their turn. They seemed much smaller than those she'd seen in her yard at home.

"Okay, as I see it, we actually have two mysteries— what happened to Jeremy Griffin and why did Cyrus Griffin leave Devon, change his name and go to London?" He opened his notebook to an empty page ready to jot down anything they found or needed to conform. "I know you're more concerned about Jeremy, but I find the whole thing very intriguing."

He'd woken three hours after a needed nap and Tessa had found his tousled appearance rather appealing. Refreshed after an early lunch he was eager to get to their work, yet in the back of her mind, niggling at her thoughts was the report from Keefer. Was Wes going to sabotage their findings or was he sincere in helping her with this research? Time would tell, and she would remain wary.

"It is," she agreed. "Let's recap what we have so far."

They sat side by side at the cottage computer, waiting for the genealogy site to come up. Wes opened the page with their research on his laptop which he had placed next to the computer.

The office nook consisted of a six-foot wooden table with two chairs stolen from the main dining table. Behind them and lining the north wall next to the window with the feeder entertainment was a shelving unit that had been built to fit the space. Occupying the shelves were mostly books referring to antiques, history and genealogy. She glanced at the titles as Wes readied himself. "Was your grandfather interested in history as well?"

He followed her gaze and shook his head softly. "No, these are mine. He was more interested in fishing, woodworking and animals. He built this cottage and the furniture in it back in the sixties."

"Here it is." he said, returning to their task. "You found Josias Griffin's military records in India: died unmarried, no apparent heirs." He jotted a note about Wilson Griffin. "We need to confirm that Wilson's son died in WWII and that he was his only child. Just as a curiosity I'd like to see Wilson's marriage certificate and see what facts are on it." A thought suddenly occurred to him. "We need to search for all information regarding the two Fenwick boys, because if we find them after Alexander Fenwick changed his name then we will know we have the wrong family. So why don't I search for them in subsequent years on the '91 and '01 census records to begin with and you see if you can find anything on Jeremy Fenwick."

"All right, I'll start with the 1891 census, then I'll look for a marriage or military records."

They worked companionably each searching on their own web site looking for proof that the Fenwick boys were in fact Cyrus Griffin's sons. Tessa checked for the ten-year-old Jeremy Fenwick. She found ten, in all of England with the right age but none in Devon. Then she widened her search by leaving out the age and was rewarded with two in Devon. One had the wrong age, transcribed as one instead of eleven.

"Here, look at this!" Tessa had found Jeremy Fenwick living in Exeter. "Jeremy Fenwick adopted son of Doctor Harold Witherspoon, aged eleven, born in Devon."

"Wow, a doctor. He was a very lucky boy." He rewarded the find with a glowing smile. "Now just to make sure, look for the doctor in Devon on the '81 census."

"Okay." She saved Jeremy Fenwick's page then searched for the Witherspoon family in Devonport. Harold Witherspoon lived with his wife Cecelia, two children, and his new born son aged one month. Why the baby hadn't shown up on the next census was obvious after she checked deaths for that year and found a two-month-old baby named Witherspoon who had died in Devonport.

"I wonder what the connection was between Alexander Fenwick and Doctor Witherspoon?"

Wes fished through the documents that Tessa had printed out the day before. The '81 census had listed Alexander Fenwick as a servant. "Maybe he worked for the doctor."

"After losing their son so young, his wife would certainly be able to care for an infant." She sighed thinking of the dual tragedy. "It's nice that they let him keep his last name."

"They must have been kind people." Wes checked the clock in the kitchen. They'd been working for four hours. His grandmother was beginning to prep for supper. "I'd better help Nan with the bar-b-cue."

Tessa sat on the front deck overlooking the lake as Wes cleaned and fired up the ancient cast-iron bar-b-cue.

It wasn't a large lake compared to others in Ontario, but the many small islands and bays gave it an appearance of being larger than most. Nan's home, for it was too spacious and well built to be a cottage in Tessa's mind, sat up on a ridge of land that surrounded the southern end of the lake.

Log steps, dug into the earth made their way from the front deck down to the lake shore and a huge dock that had been built on large squares of floating foam.

Wes noticed her gaze as he finished up his scraping with the wire brush then lit the burners. "Tony and I built the dock two summers ago. The old one was small and the main structure rotten; too unsafe." It was a T-shaped dock that provided a protected area for the sixteen-foot aluminum boat that was now tied along the short side while also providing a large area from which to swim or relax on deck chairs. The four deck chairs lining the edge of the shore were the old-fashioned Adirondack style, each one painted in a bright colour.

A squirrel chattered at them obviously displeased with the new arrivals. It was a northern red squirrel, small compared with the greys of the city. He chattered then quieted when he found a peanut that Nan had tossed earlier that day. He quickly moved to one of his secret caches and began to bury his find. "Wes, look." Tessa had noticed a blue jay in a tree above the squirrel's stash, watching, unseen as the squirrel busily buried his find. Wes joined her on the deck bench and watched as the drama was about to unfold.

The squirrel climbed an adjacent tree and sat sprawled on a branch overlooking his hidden treasures. Suddenly the blue jay swooped down and with a few quick probes with his beak found the peanut and triumphantly took it back to a tree limb near by and began pounding it against the branch with his beak. The squirrel had watched all of this and now sat in his tree protesting this thievery, unable to do much about it; while the blue jay, ignoring all, extracted the last peanut then flew off.

Wes watched with interest. "This happens a lot, but he'll get more; Nan has a jar full of peanuts. They don't go hungry."

It was nearing six o'clock and the lake had calmed after a light wind during the day. It was also midweek, so the lake was relatively free of the boisterous weekend crowd. "How about a boat ride after supper?"

"I'd like that."

Supper conversation revolved around chores and items Nan needed repaired or attended to. There was a leak in the caulking around the living room window, Nan had found two shingles that had blown off the roof after the last wind storm a month ago, that needed to be checked, and the remainder of the cottage needed to be painted after Tony had started on the back of the home. There was a large store of chopped wood that was piled and ran along the side of Nan's garden, but more would be needed for the winter to come. Power outages were common, and the family always made sure that heat was available if the electricity failed.

The breeze calmed after supper and the lake was as smooth as glass with only the occasional ripple. The sixteen-foot aluminum boat was used mostly for fishing and as such had the appropriate necessities. There was an agreed upon ban on Jet-Skis and motors over 40hp, explained Wes. "People like to come up here for peace and quiet, and with a small lake like this, noise affects most of the people living here."

They sat side by side as Wes guided the boat around islands and along the shoreline. "Are there many cottages on the lake?"

Wes noticed her observing the larger areas of vacant land between the buildings. "Average, I guess, although many people in the '60s, when the land became available, bought double lots. Since then, the owners have formed a corporation and agreed to a few simple rules which allow enjoyment for all. There are four lakes that are part of the corporation. The smallest one about two miles away allow non-motorized boats only."

There was a bridge where the upper lake joined the larger lower lake. A store stood at the junction of the two lakes providing mostly fast foods and sundry items.

With a sky void of cloud, the water reflected the blue above, a deep blue that sparkled in the sunlight as their boat broke the surface. It was a wonderful day and Tessa took a moment to reflect upon her guide. There was something different about him away from the academia of the library. He seemed at home here, rugged and confident in his surroundings. Maybe it was his unshaven appearance, Tessa wasn't sure, maybe she had been too wrapped up in her work to actually see Wes for who he was, but she found Wes to be an attractive, kind man, someone she would like to get to know better. Yet Keefer's words came back to her, forcing her to face the reality that Wes was working for an unscrupulous man and had most likely offered to help her with her search; with the goal of misleading and delaying any find she might have found on her own.

She wondered if she should come right out and

confront him. Would he be truthful about his client?

"Look, over there!"

She followed the direction he pointed and saw a deer at the edge of the lake, drinking, as if humans nearby were not a threat. Wes slowed the motor to an idle then turned it off completely when the deer raised its head noticing them. "There are quite a few deer in the area. I guess they feel safe here."

The water lapped gently at the hull, as their boat drifted, the waves of their path now engulfing them. They had entered the upper lake now and for the moment theirs was the only boat on the lake that they could see. An island ahead of them, covered with fir and pine trees enhanced the illusion that they were alone in a forested wilderness. He smiled sheepishly at her. "I'm glad you took my offer to come here." The sky was beginning to take on a pinkish glow in the west as the sun slipped behind the hills and trees that obscured the horizon. "That first day, after you left, I wondered if I'd see you again."

Tessa wondered what he would have done if she hadn't returned to the library. Was there someone else from his firm poised, ready to take up the hunt if he had failed. Someone who had followed her from Hannah's home?

"I guess we can thank Kevin Fairchild for that. If he

hadn't dismissed my company and my research, I wouldn't have been so determined to investigate further." She watched Wes's face as she said the name of the lawyer hoping for some sign of recognition, some slip that would confirm his motive, but there was none.

"Well, I'm glad he did, and I'm glad you came back to the library." He looked at the night sky gauging the time before darkness would cover the lake. "I think we have time; I want to show you the falls." It wasn't far, perhaps five minutes more. The falls, were really just a group of large rocks positioned at the end of the lake that allowed the water from a nearby creek, to cascade gracefully into the smaller lake. Tessa watched from the boat as water gurgled over the grey granite. Perhaps rapids would be a better name for the formation.

Wes positioned their boat along the shore where the water was less disturbed by the falling water. He held the boat snugly against the shore inviting Tessa to get out with his outstretched right arm. There was strength and muscle in that arm as Tessa held on, stepping carefully onto the slippery rocks along the water line. "Thank you." she said shyly, suddenly realizing that this was the first time she had touched him. Wes hadn't seemed to notice the effect he had made and quickly tied the boat to an embedded tree stump before it swerved out into the lake.

"Up here."

Chapter 8

They faced the lake with the fire before them. The moon, clear now of the few clouds that threatened to cover it as they drove back in the last light of the setting sun. Wes had shown her his favourite spot above the rapids, a place where the wild life of the lake felt safer away from the ever-present cottagers. Here they'd watched as a raccoon family enjoyed the gurgling waters while they ventured into the shallow areas along the edge. The younger ones splashing while the mother kept a wary eye out for danger.

Nan had brought down a snack once she saw they had returned to the dock from their ride.

"Here, you take this one. It's not as burned as yours." Wes surrounded the roasted wiener with a soft bun and pulled it from the pointed sapling he used for roasting hotdogs.

Tessa smiled, looking at her attempt at cooking over an open fire. "Gladly, thanks." Sizzling and blackened from having her food too close to the flames, she handed her stick to Wes in exchange for the delicious looking hotdog.

Moonlight shone across the lake adding sparkle to the already dark waters. A slight breeze gave the water a flickering movement. Something small scurried near them at the waters edge. Further up the lake something gave a frightened cry as if suddenly aware of a predator. There was a splash then silence.

"So, what's our plan for tomorrow?"

"Well, in the morning I'm going to finish painting the house while you search. I would start with Alexander Fenwick's first marriage and then check for Jeremy's birth records. See if you can find parish records. On line will work for now but you'll need to get official documents later once you have everything figured out."

Tessa looked up. The sky was clear of cloud and the stars were more numerous than she had ever remembered seeing them. They sat in companionable silence enjoying their food and the night sounds of the forest. "It's beautiful up here. Thank you for inviting me."

Wes smiled, pleased that she was enjoying something he loved. "There's still a lot of work to be done. Do you find yourself thinking about them? I know I do when I'm hunting my ancestors."

In truth Tessa had been thinking about Wes. His strong arm as he helped her out of the boat, the softness of his hand as he took hers when they crossed a rocky path along the rapids. "Yes," she lied. "I just can't figure out why Alexander would change his name and travel so far with his two sons and leave an infant behind. Okay, I can see him leaving for a better job, but why change his name?"

"Well, people usually change their name for two reasons. One, they don't like it. Maybe it's too ethnic sounding. A lot of people changed their German sounding names during World War One."

Tessa thought about that, and indeed she did know of a friend of a friend who had changed her name for that reason. "Yes, but Cyrus changed his first name too."

"That leads me then to two, they're hiding from some one or some thing for whatever reason. I'd bet on two." He suddenly pointed upward. "Look, a shooting star."

Tessa glanced upward just as the tail end disappeared over the tree horizon. "Something else has been bothering me."

"What's that?"

"I'm not sure now that the two families are one in the same. Cyrus was wealthy, and Alexander was a servant. In all other ways they appear to be the same, yet this is a big difference to explain."

Wes leaned back in his chair and looked up. "Sometimes you can find out a lot by searching lateral connections as well, maybe something will click and fit it all together. Check out his wife and her family. Why didn't he leave Jeremy with one of them or his own family? Also see what he was doing in 1871."

"Okay, I'll start on that tomorrow."

"Oh, and you might also look for any newspaper events around the time he left and see if something influenced his move to London."

Tessa had been jotting down notes as Wes proposed her plan of attack. She wondered now how Wes would suppress her findings, then felt ashamed of her thoughts. So far Wes had been only supportive and helpful and so far, she didn't see any signs of misdirection from his suggestions. Maybe Keefer was wrong. Maybe he had looked up the wrong person, although that didn't seem likely. For now, finding Jeremy was her foremost goal, although the mystery of Cyrus Griffin nagged at her thoughts.

It was four-thirty and Wes and Tessa had spent the afternoon apart, each working on their self-assigned task. Wes was finishing up the house painting while Tessa had only touched the surface of her investigation finding more questions than answers. She had found Alexander Fenwick's marriage in 1875 in Exeter to Mary Ann Tyrell, but after checking the parish document she noticed that he had put down a different name for his father than he had on his second marriage papers. She wondered if that fact was enough to disqualify her findings?

After three hours of checking all of Wes's favourite sites, Tessa had noted some success. There was a tap on the outside of the screened window next to her. "How's it going?" Wes had finished painting the wooden siding that covered that end of the house and was now painting the trim its contrasting colour.

"Quite well actually. Do you remember that visitor on the 1881 census that was listed with Alexander and the three boys? Well turns out that Alexander's wife and James Tyrell are related. By his age I figured Mary Ann Tyrell and he were brother and sister." Wes gave her a look that said, 'prove it'. "I had to go back to the '61 census to find her family. Her father was a mariner, Nicholas Tyrell, and they had four children, Mary Ann and James among them."

"Well done! Anything else?"

"I'm not too sure if this makes a difference, but the name Alexander gave for his father differs from the one Cyrus had on his second marriage certificate." She pulled out the page with a rough chart for Alexander Fenwick, "It's down as, William."

"Well, if he didn't want to be found it makes sense to change his family history."

"I was able to find the Fenwick family on the 1861 census: William, his wife Caroline, and seven children; Alexander being the second youngest. And his birth year matches that of Cyrus.

Tessa shuffled through the pages she had sorted according to names of those she searched for. "Here, I also found Alexander Fenwick on the '71 census working for a Thomas Witherspoon as a servant, he was seventeen. So, thinking there could be a connection. I did as you suggested and looked for Thomas Witherspoon in the 1881 census, and guess what?"

Wes paused his painting, enjoying her enthusiasm. "What?" He waited for her to reveal her discovery.

"Thomas lived in Exeter with his wife and one son, and he lived up the street from Harold Witherspoon. The last name was difficult to read which is why I couldn't find him at first, but the family was the same."

Proud of herself, she smiled triumphantly at Wes. "So, there's our link to the good doctor."

"Wow, I'm impressed."

"How's the painting coming along?"

It was a sunny day and Wes looked warm and tired. "Once I finish this window, I'm done for the day. I won't be long. After supper we can work on it together."

Supper was a welcome change from researching and the conversation revolved around plans for tomorrow. Nan would be off early in the morning to spend a day or two with an ailing friend. Wes would work on the roof repair and Tessa would continue where she left off.

Nan had put a paper plate with spaghetti left-overs on it, on the ground in the back yard. Tessa had been curious as to why, then with Nan and Wes, watched as the biggest, fluffiest skunk she had ever seen, waddled out from under Wes's SUV. It dragged the plate slowly back until the plate and skunk were safely under the protection of the vehicle. The back-door light was on and shone just enough light that occasionally the skunk could be seen with strands of pasta hanging from its mouth.

"I never knew skunks would eat spaghetti."

Nan nodded, smiling as the animal enjoyed his treat. "This one seems to like it very much. Sometimes when I'm here alone, I make enough for him and myself. Sometimes I'll open the back door and watch through the storm-door window."

As odd as that sounded, Tessa understood. She smiled

at Nan's child-like enthusiasm for this small creature then continued watching the show.

Later they sat at the table the drapes drawn back so they could see the rain as it fell softly on the foliage surrounding the cottage. They sat side by side sharing the notes Tessa had made so both could check what had been discovered so far.

Wes had a research sheet he had made up for keeping track of the progress they were making. It listed the required documents and proof they needed for each person they were looking for. Once a fact was found the source was written beside it, so the required documents could be acquired later.

Nan sat in her recliner working on an afghan she was knitting for her bed. "I'm going to make some hot chocolate. Would either of you like some?" After getting a nod from both her guests Nan set her knitting aside and went to make the warm drinks.

Chapter 9

Tessa lay in her bed. She had been woken by the drumming of a woodpecker on the tree outside her window. She knew it was early by the light that filtered in through the glass but confirmed it by checking the clock next to her bed. Six in the morning wasn't too early for some people, and Tessa could hear Wes and Nan as they prepared for the day. She lay under the covers thinking. Why was it important to her to find Hannah's uncle? Why was she going to all this trouble? Why not just let the lawyer deal with things?

She knew. Not just because she had promised Hannah but because she had a gut feeling that something wasn't on the up and up. Everything was too pat; the lawyer suddenly finding an heir. No, she would continue till the end, even if she didn't find an heir, she had to try.

The wind blew the leaves on the tree and the light dimmed as clouds forecast a threat of rain. She could hear the shower running and decided to stay in bed until her alarm went off at seven-thirty.

By seven-thirty drizzle had started its gentle fall on the foliage and made a soft dripping sound as it fell from the leaves on to the ground beside her room. The sky had darkened, and it seemed Wes would have to wait for his roof repair and hope it wasn't too late. Nan had left, and Wes was in the kitchen preparing breakfast as Tessa emerged from her room ready to start the day.

"So, you cook too?"

Wes smiled. "Just the basics." He stood by the stove wrapping the bacon he had just fried, in a paper towel. "Bacon, eggs, toast, coffee, juice. How do you like your eggs?"

"Scrambled."

"I was hoping you'd say that. I usually break the yolk when I try fried." He gave a shrug as he looked to the window. "Looks like a long grey day ahead. Hopefully it won't rain too hard until I get a chance to check out the roof for leaks." He nodded toward the two buckets Nan kept by the window in case of leaks. He divided the scrambled eggs onto the two plates then shared out the bacon before bringing them to the table with the freshly buttered toast. Tessa enjoyed her breakfast then admitted to Wes that she actually preferred easy-over fried eggs, something she could dip her bacon into. He had laughed and promised them for tomorrow.

By eight-thirty the clouds threatening a further heavy rain had moved off to the east. Tessa could hear the ladder as it settled against the far side of the house. Noise of Wes's shoes echoed through the ceiling above her as he walked. After a day away, it was time to check in with Keefer. She turned on her cell phone. Reception was sketchy so far north and she waited until the connection counters showed on the screen. The cloud cover seemed to have helped. There were two messages since her last time using the phone. Wes was still on the roof, so she clicked on the message icon. Both were from Keefer. The first one was a simple 'call me!' phrase, that by its simplicity implied urgency. She checked the second message anticipating the explanation and saw in it what she had been dreading, 'the lawyer has just announced to the media that he has found Hannah's heir'.

Wes's footsteps sounded above her as she read Keefer's message. She had time and felt sure she couldn't be overheard. Tessa dialed quickly. She waited for what seemed minutes and no answer. The sound of a hammer on the roof got her attention. It looked as though Wes had found where the shingles had been damaged. With no answer from Keefer, she decided to message him quickly. 'Found Cyrus Griffin in 1881 Devon aka Alexander Fenwick. See what you can dig up on why he might have changed his name when he left. Have found his son Jeremy and will continue to pursue this family.' Then as an after thought she added, 'Wes has been very helpful. Are you sure about him and who he works for?'

Tessa turned off her phone and sat for a moment looking at the research papers before her on the makeshift computer table. She had only a few days left before it might become too late. She turned on her laptop and waited dutifully. The screen remained black with a message that said, 'no service available'.

On the floor to her left where Wes usually sat was Nan's tower computer. Tessa pressed the on button then waited for the monitor screen to come on. Same message; 'no service available'. There was some more banging above her as Wes tacked on more tiles over the defective ones. She knew there was a satellite dish on that end of the house. Could that be why the computers didn't work? Tessa knew next to little about how satellite dishes worked or what they controlled in a household. Was it just a coincidence that Wes was working near where the dish was attached and now there was no internet service? Her cellphone worked but that was through a different satellite service. Was this how Wes intended to derail her; stop her from finding the truth? The hammering on the roof had stopped now and Tessa could hear the ladder as it was being taken down. She still had her phone and if forced to she could still access the same genealogical sites, although it would be more difficult without the larger screen and the use of multiple windows.

The sound of Wes coming in the back door distracted her. "Well, I found the one leak that was causing Nan all the problems by the window. There were a couple of missing shingles just above the window wall. Water was getting down the plywood joint and running along the two-by-four." He picked at some beads of silicone that had stuck to his hands while repairing the damage. "It should last until Nan gets the roof done again." He smiled warmly at Tessa seated at the computer table. "Found out anything new?"

Tessa shook her head and shrugged. "The internet is out." She waited for a reaction to her news. "Could it be the dish?"

"No, the dish doesn't control the internet. It's probably the router. It needs resetting every so often." He finished wiping his hands. "Don't know why, but it's easy to fix." He walked over to the shelf by the kitchen. The lights across part of the front were red. He switched the router off, waited a few seconds then turned it back on. "There you are, it won't take long."

"Thank you." She smiled hoping it didn't look forced. She was ashamed now at her mistrust of him and felt a renewed confidence in their effort. "I'll wait for you to join me."

"I better change out of these work clothes. Hate silicon, no matter how hard I try, it gets everywhere." He peeled the last bit from his fingers then went to change.

It wasn't long before Wes had taken his seat next to Tessa. He'd changed into his jeans and blue, plaid flannel shirt. He stood up abruptly and took Tessa's hand, indicating she stand too. "Before we start to work there's something I need to say." When Tessa didn't respond, he continued. "I would like very much to kiss you first." Then suddenly aware of how this might be taken, he added, "If that's all right with you?"

Tessa smiled at his awkwardness, then nodded. "Perfectly." At which moment he surrounded her with his arms, drawing her near, then kissed her. His lips were warm and soft and passionate, compelling Tessa to return the gesture.

"It's definitely better when you participate too." He smiled shyly then released her from his embrace.

Tessa's head was swimming. Her legs were weak, and she felt a sudden urge to kiss Wes again. She tried to calm herself. When she was able to think straight again, she looked at Wes directly as they took their chairs again. "Who do you work for? And don't tell me you're a teacher because I know different."

This certainly wasn't what Wes expected after a romantic moment. He was quiet. Tessa wondered if he was trying to think up a defence for his betrayal. He looked into her eyes then spoke just one word— "Duffy".

"It's true I took time from work, and I was working on my family genealogy when I met you, but it was Duffy who told me you were going to the library."

This was more than Tessa could put together. Her suspicions verified, she had one main question to clear up. "How did Duffy know about you?"

Wes gave her a sheepish look. "He's, my godfather. My grandfather and Duffy were best friends. Nan and Duffy have kept in touch over the years, and when he realized what Hannah's lawyer was up to, he called me to see if I could help. I didn't expect to find you. But I'm glad how it turned out."

Tessa, her skepticism appeased, had a final question. "Why didn't you or Duffy tell me?"

"I guess he didn't know for sure if you would follow through and thought it better if I help and encourage your search instead. After you questioned him about the lawyer and missing paperwork, he thought it better if no one knew he was involved: being a beneficiary himself—it might be construed as jealousy."

Chapter 10

They spent the rest of the afternoon hunting for Jeremy Fenwick. The weather had finally delivered on its promise of rain, and Tessa listened to the downpour that had suddenly invaded the area. Wes was by the window checking for leaks when the first loud clap of thunder rolled across the lake, as a jagged lightening streak lit up the sky like an old-fashioned camera bulb. He touched the upper part of the window and feeling no wetness nodded to Tessa. "Looks like the patching will hold."

The sky was dark with cloud, back-lit by another crack of lightening, as the thunder boomed above them. The lights flickered then went out. Both laptop and computer screens went black and there was a moment of uncertainty as to whether the lights would stay off or come back on. Rain hit the front windows with renewed force as the storm seemed to stall over the lake and the lights stayed off. "We'll probably need a fire. The phone line will be out too for a while, does your cell work?"

Tessa turned on her cell and waited for the swipe page to come up. It did but it showed no reception counters. "No, not now."

"Don't you own a cell phone?"

"I use to, or rather I do, but when I'm on vacation I don't." He busied himself in the kitchen as he spoke. "I will again when I go back to work. I was beginning to be too dependent and enslaved by my phone, so I decided to give it up for a few weeks."

He rummaged through a few drawers under the counter. "Well at least we'll have some light as it gets darker. No telling how long the power will be off. Nan has some candles here somewhere." He held up three well used candles triumphantly, their sides covered in lumpy spilled wax from previous use. "These should do nicely."

Tessa listened as the storm continued, showing no intention of leaving. She tried to count the seconds between the flashes and the pounding bang of the thunder. There were none as both happened almost simultaneously, confirming that the storm was directly above them.

Luckily there was a supply of dry firewood in the cottage. Wes's grandfather had built a bench along the window side of the house where one could recline and watch the lake. Inside the bench, under the hinged lids was where wood was kept, dry and out of the way until needed. Wes removed the cushions and drew out enough kindling and logs to get a fire going. He tossed Tessa the matches and asked her to set up the candles. After twenty minutes of preparation Wes and Tessa were sitting comfortably on a couch before the fire with candles at either end resting on end tables and one in the kitchen.

"I guess its hotdogs again for supper."

"That sound great. I'll do better this time."

"I should hope so after all your experience." They laughed. "I think Nan has some wine stored away." He went to look for the wine while Tessa set up a seventies-style, metal, TV tray to the side of the fireplace to hold their dishes and hotdog condiments. Another crack of lightening lit up the night sky. This time the thunder hesitated a moment before the rumbling that followed which meant the storm was moving off slowly.

"Here, I found it. Is red, okay?"

"Well, I'm not sure, are hotdogs considered red or white meat?"

Wes looked at the package of wieners with feigned scrutiny. "They're all beef, so we're good." Wes carried the wine and glasses back to the impromptu dinner space while Tessa brought the food.

Two hours later they were sitting on the couch enjoying

the rest of their wine. The storm had passed and shortly after the lights had come back on making the printer go through its chorus of strange start-up noises. Enjoying the firelight and candles the two preferred to sit in darkness continuing to enjoy the fire and candlelight. Tessa took a sip of her wine, then twisted around to face Wes, his arm dislodged by her movement. "So, what does the dish do?"

He snorted softly. "Well, nothing really; it's not hooked up." He stroked her hair as Tessa leaned back, her head now on his lap. "My grandfather was in the Korean war. I guess because of that he only slept a few hours at a time. Back when they first had the cottage I remember coming up and finding their television hooked up by coat hangers and wires to the curtain rod. There were only a few channels back then that you could get here and half of those had so much static it was like watching a snowstorm. But he had no problem sleeping while watching the snowy screen, listening to the static." He laughed remembering. "In fact, if you turned it off, he'd suddenly wake up, protesting. Anyway, when dishes came out Nan bought one for him. It was great ... no more noisy snow on the screen."

He took another sip of wine. Tessa took his glass and set it on the floor beside the couch, the empty glass sparkled, reflecting the golden flames of the fire. She took his hand in hers. "So where is the TV?"

"After Grandad died, Nan took the TV away and discontinued the dish service. I guess it brought back too many memories and was a constant reminder that she was alone now."

"It must have been hard for her."

"Yes, for the first couple of years, but she's fine now."

They enjoyed the firelight in companionable silence for a while. "What are you thinking?" he asked.

"I'm worried about the lawyer. He's named an heir and I'm worried we'll be too late."

"I have a friend named Moose, well, his name is really George, but his friends call him Moose."

"Moose?" Tessa tried to imagine what a man named 'Moose' would look like. "Why, because of his size?"

"Not moose the animal, mousse the hair product." He laughed at the look on her face. "No, it's because when he was younger, he always used too much hair cream. He ended up looking like a sleazy gangster from the thirties. Although now out of respect for him, we spell it like the animal, but it's an inside joke and all his friends know the real reason for his nickname."

"So, what does this have to do with my situation?" She'd realized by now that Wes liked to tell stories and elaborate where he could on interesting details.

"Moose was the executor for his great-grandfather. The will was fairly straight forward, and he thought it would be finalized in a couple of weeks. But as it turned out it took over a year."

This peeked Tessa's interest. "Why?"

"His uncle had some investments and once that was figured out, they had to wait until his final tax return was done. So, I think you have more time than you thought."

She stroked his hand. "I'm glad to hear that, even if it did take a round-about route." Tessa laughed. "Okay, we have some time. I think we did well today, we've figured out where Jeremy Fenwick isn't."

They had worked together several hours before the storm. There were four possible Jeremy Fenwicks on the 1901 census, none of which were in Devon and none that seemed right. Two were in Yorkshire, one in Kent, and one in Warwickshire. All had been close in age, but none were listed as being born in Devon. Each record had been painstakingly scrutinized. One, a navy seaman, had a wife and child. Two lived with their parents and the last was in an asylum. "I suppose he could be one of them," Tessa had suggested. So, they decided to keep these as possible leads and names to eliminate in the future. They even checked possible death records for a Jeremy Fenwick and found nothing that matched. It had taken a while to make sure before moving on to a hunch Wes had.

They checked for the Witherspoon family and eventually found them living in Cornwall, near the Devon border. Listed as their son, was Jeremy Witherspoon. Had Jeremy changed his name once he became old enough? Now they had two last names to look for on further records making things a bit more complicated, but at least now they could discard the four Jeremy Fenwicks they had found earlier as the one they were seeking.

By four o'clock they were looking into the 1911 census records for both Jeremy Fenwick and Jeremy Witherspoon. The navy seaman Jeremy now had four children. The asylum inmate was still confined and of the two that had been living with their parents, one had died, and one had married a girl from Ireland. But their Jeremy Fenwick was nowhere to be found. Once again, they checked for the Witherspoon family and found that they had moved back to Exeter minus their children.

"What were the names of the Witherspoon children?" asked Wes, obviously thinking laterally again.

Tessa flipped through her notebook and found the relevant information. "Harold Jr., who was two years older than Jeremy and Ann who was the eldest."

"Here, I found Harold Witherspoon, he's living in London." He waited as the 1911 census transcription page loaded. Harold Witherspoon was living in a Kensington home with his two children. listing him as a widower. Living with them was his brother Jeremy Trenmate, his wife Emily and three children.

Tessa leaned closer to read the names. "What kind of name is Trenmate?"

Wes shrugged, puzzled. "None, that I've heard of. Let's check the actual document." Wes leaned closer as the screen showing the census record came up.

"Did you know that the 1911 census records are the first available records actually written by our ancestors? Prior to that year all household schedules were destroyed after copied by the enumerator."

Harold Witherspoon and family came up as transcribed, but the second family was more difficult to decipher. The writing had two ink smudges and some of the letters were more difficult to make out; the handwriting was very vertical making letters such as; m, n, u, w, all look similar. "I must say Harold's handwriting isn't the easiest to read."

"Can you enlarge it?" He waited as Tessa expanded the lettering.

"Look, the 'T' and 'r' are actually part of the same letter. And the 'e' at the end could easily be part of the 't', making it a 'k'. This has to be him."

"It looks like 'Fenwick' to me. I wonder why the transcriber had difficulty? Can we prove it?"

"Yes. We check for a marriage between Jeremy and Emily. Then we check for the birth records of the three kids and verify the last name." He smiled at their progress as the first rain of the storm fell.

That had been several hours ago. Tessa looked up at Wes from her position on the couch. The light from the fire, flickered and gave the room a warm glow. The candles had long since extinguished themselves as the wicks burned themselves to the bottom. After an afternoon of working together, she now felt comfortable with this new relationship.

Chapter 11

The storm had lasted throughout the evening and tapered off into the night, and Tessa woke to the sound of collective drops as they fell onto the roof from leaves outside her window. There was a sound of a ladder tapping against the front of the cottage. It was eight o'clock and Wes—obviously an early riser—had intentions of finishing up his painting job. There was a small part left to do that shouldn't take more than an hour, so Tessa decided to get up and make breakfast for the two of them.

She thought about their evening together during the storm and couldn't remember a more wonderful time. Wes had explained his connection to Duffy, and she was now secure in his help. She wondered where this relationship would end up and smiled to herself.

There was a tap at the kitchen window. "What's so amusing?" he asked.

"You, you have paint in your hair."

He brushed his hair back with his free arm and smiled back. "How long till breakfast?"

Tessa placed the long strips of bacon into the pan. Then plugged the coffee pot into the outlet by the stove. "Fifteen minutes?" He nodded agreement then resumed his work; a little faster than before, she noticed.

Their breakfast was a repeat of the one he had made only this time Tessa had made fried eggs. Wes took his place at the table ready to enjoy a well-deserved meal. There was a sudden sound of bells. "Is that your phone?"

"Sounds like it." Tessa went to the side table by the fire where she had left her phone last night. "Hello? Sorry, I haven't been able to get reception well."

Wes noticed her voice suddenly change to one of concern. "What? When?" He waited, and watched as her face expressed disbelief. "Thank you for calling me. Okay. Bye."

"Tessa, what is it?" She came back to the table, a dazed look upon her face. She lay the phone down beside her plate, then looked at Wes as she sat.

"Keefer's dead. A hit and run." She shook her head slowly. "He was helping me look into Cyrus Griffin and Alexander Fenwick." Her eyes suddenly grew teary. "We've worked together on a few cases and he found this one interesting and wanted to help." Then a thought occurred to her. "You don't think there's a connection?"

"Because he was looking into Cyrus Griffin? How would anyone know he was helping you?" Wes reasoned.

"Unless they don't know, and someone thought he was just getting too nosey. Or maybe it's just what it seems, an accident."

Then a thought occurred to Wes. "Who was it that phoned you?"

"Hanley, from the office," she said, thinking now what Wes was thinking. "Keefer was *my* source. No one at the firm knew him. I may have mentioned a Keefer, but how would they know that the Adam Keefer who was killed was my Keefer?" She paused, now wondering if she and Wes might be in danger. "I think I might have made a mistake in acknowledging the news. What can we do?"

The breakfast long forgotten; Wes put his hand over hers. "You forget, I have my sources too."
She smiled for the calmness he meant to convey. "Did you mention to anyone where you were going?"

"No, *I* didn't even know where we were going."

"Did you mention my name to anyone who would be able to find out where I worked or who I was?"

"Just Keefer." She looked sheepishly at Wes. "It was Keefer who alerted me as to who you were. He always worked alone."

Wes gave her a look then nodded in agreement.

"You're safe here for the meantime, so let's wait here and continue our research. I'll call a few people to look into Keefer's death." He looked down at his breakfast, cold now since the phone call. "For now, there's nothing to be done but finish our breakfast." He picked up his plate and walked over to the small microwave Nan kept on the sideboard. "Ten seconds should be enough." He gave her a reassuring smile. "Don't worry."

After breakfast, and after Wes cleaned up his painting materials, they set together at the computer table determined now to find out what happened to Jeremy Fenwick. Tessa, distracted by events, had difficulty attending to her task: finding the marriage of Jeremy Fenwick and Emily.

It was a sunny morning now and those creatures who had sheltered during the rain now ventured out to lead their usual lives. She could see the humming birds at their feeder. The red squirrel stretched out in the sun on a nearby branch. Bumble bees buzzed around their favourite summer blooms, and she realized how life goes on, eventually abandoning those who fall away. Keefer had been a friend and she felt a sorrow she hadn't expected to feel. He was the first person in her life who had died since she was little: she had few memories of her great-grandmother's funeral. Keefer left behind a wife and two

100

children and she sat next to Wes imagining the pain they must be feeling.

He reached over and put a reassuring arm around her shoulder. He closed out his email page and loaded his favourite genealogy site. "There, I've emailed both Tony and Moose and filled them in on what we're doing. Hopefully I'll hear back in a day or two."

"What can they do?" she asked, skeptical of their possible assistance.

"I forgot to tell you," he said, anticipating her reaction. "My brother actually is a criminal lawyer, and Moose, he's a private detective. He used to work under cover and still has many friends and connections on the Toronto police force."

He checked the window on her laptop and notice the large Google logo on her page. "Why don't you start with Ancestry while I search for the baptisms on my site."

She smiled back and nodded, determined to finish their search, one way or another.

It didn't take very long. "Here." She underlined the entry with her finger, as Wes watched with her while the page came up. "We're lucky, it's the parish record."

Jeremy Fenwick was married to Emily Stockton April 28, 1902, in the parish church of the Holy Trinity in the City of

Exeter, after banns; ironically, the same church his father had been married in. Both were single, and both could write their names. Under the heading of Father's name and occupation, Jeremy had named doctor, Harold Witherspoon.

"So, it seems that whoever filled in the 1901 census forms for the family didn't know Jeremy was adopted or he may have just taken the doctor's name through school." suggested Tessa.

"I guess it doesn't matter much now that we have our link to the Witherspoons." He pointed to the two witnesses listed: Harold Witherspoon and possibly his sister Ann Robinson. "It would be easier if we had some adoption records, but formal legal adoptions didn't start until the 1920s so there may not even be any."

Tessa was starting to feel overwhelmed by all the circumstantial evidence. She believed they now had all the information needed to connect all three brothers. Wes had concluded that the Fenwick sons—Josias and Wilson—didn't appear to exist after 1881 and Alexander Fenwick himself had disappeared from paper history.

"I need to summarize what we've found so far." She sorted out her notes according to dates. "Alexander's parents were William and Caroline Fenwick. We've found William

Fenwick and his family on the '61 census. Alexander is shown as age seven along with six other children." She looked at Wes for confirmation. "And I realize that besides on-line documents I must also get official documents where I can and also use the parish registers, but I think we have enough proof at the moment to continue." She pulled out a rough chart she had made with names scribbled down as they were found.

"Now, Alexander married Mary Ann Tyrell in 1875 in Exeter. They had three children: Jo, Wil and Jeremy. We have now found these birth records, both at the parish level and civil registration." She smiled at their progress and gave Wes a questioning look. "Jo, Wil and Alexander seem to have disappeared after the 1881 census."

"I couldn't find anything," Wes confirmed.

She nodded in agreement. "Jeremy is on the '91 and 1901 census as son/adopted son of Harold Witherspoon. He was married in 1902, in Exeter to Emily Stockton: we found the marriage record, which proves again the Witherspoon connection. They had three children, Sarah, Emily and Harold. We've looked for Jo, Wil and Cyrus Griffin, and they don't appear to exist before the 1891 census."

Seemingly pleased with herself Tessa passed Wes the chart that incorporated their findings so far.

"Well done. Remember though that absence of evidence doesn't prove or disprove the two families are one in the same, but I think we have enough corroborative evidence to continue."

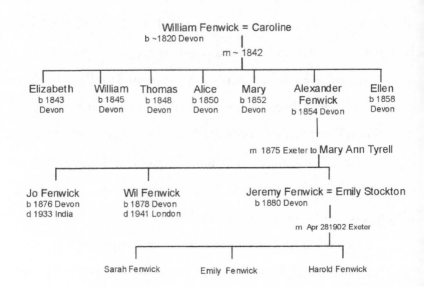

"So, I guess we trace Jeremy's family forward and see what we can find." Tessa gave Wes a concerned look. "I'm still not sure that the courts will accept our findings as enough proof that Alexander and Cyrus are the same person."

"All we can do is present the proof we've found and let them compare ours to the proof Kevin Fairchild has."

The sadness returned for a moment as she thought about her friend. "I wish I knew if Keefer found out anything."

Wes sat the chart down and wrapped his arms about Tessa. He looked into her sad eyes and gave her a reassuring hug. "We'll just have to do it on our own." Then a thought occurred to him. "What about his funeral?"

"Hanley said he wasn't sure, but probably two or three days ... I don't know." She shook her head slowly, thinking. "No one knew we were friends and I didn't know his family. If it wasn't an accident, do you think it's safe?"

"If it wasn't an accident, no,"—he pulled back enough to look in her eyes— "and that probably won't be determined unless they find the vehicle and driver. I'm still not comfortable with Hanley calling you about the accident. It appears someone knew your connection with Keefer."

Wes resumed his hug as Tessa leaned her head against his chest. "I think for your safety we should stay here and finish our work, then get Tony to check it."

Chapter 12

Tessa agreed and for the next part of the day they sat in companionable silence, each searching for their self-assigned task.

Wes felt it was important to confirm Hannah's recollection of her uncle Wil, so he carefully checked for the family and as she had told Tessa; both Wil and his wife had died during the London Blitz in 1941 and his son had died unmarried, while flying in the RAF.

By now Tessa had found all three of Jeremy's children listed in the civil registration index which later meant she could later obtain certificates if needed.

"The 1921 census records won't be out for another few years," Wes told Tessa as he noticed her scrolling through the available British census records. "So, our only help will be to find them on the 1939 Register. Fortunately, that's now available."

"What's that?"

"In anticipation of war the government took details of every civilian. It would be used to issue identity cards and organize rationing. Because the 1931 census was destroyed by fire during the war and there was no census taken during the war, the next census record available would be in1951. Luckily for us the '39 bridges that gap between '21 and '51. Without it a whole generation would be lost."

Wes switched to another site and together they looked for Jeremy's family. Tessa had already checked for Jeremy's death record and in doing so had found two of the remaining three Jeremy Fenwicks they had found in 1911. The asylum Jeremy had died just before WWI and the navy Jeremy was on the battlecruiser HMS Invincible when it was blown up by the enemy in 1916. But their Jeremy Fenwick appeared to be alive and well—if unaccounted for.

The 1939 register showed no indication of a Jeremy or Emily Fenwick. Neither had their children: Sarah, Emily or Harold been found in the register.

"So now we have to back track and start where we left off in 1911." Wes was making notes on the results of their search.

"Let's check for military records," Tessa suggested. "Jeremy would be thirty-four. Would he be too old to join up?"

Wes shook his head, wondering the same thing. "No, they took men between eighteen and forty—he might have joined up. He could also have been in the home guard."

By two, they had discovered a private Jeremy Fenwick in the Army. "Keep your fingers crossed." He smiled at her. "Many of the WWI records were lost in the bombing during WWII so we'll be lucky to find him. The ones that did survive were badly charred or had water damage and are now called the 'burnt records'." As the page loaded Wes took Tessa's left hand in his and gave it a reassuring squeeze. "We're getting closer."

He looked into her blue eyes, eager in the hunt, bright now with anticipation. Gone now was the glistening sadness they had shown earlier. He pulled her close and kissed her as the attestation record for a Jeremy Fenwick appeared.

"It's him! Look!" Written in the space beside 'next of kin' was the name—Emily Fenwick. She smiled, excited that they had found him, then in a sudden moment she said, worried, "Do you think he survived?" Jeremy had joined the Grenadier Guards, an infantry regiment that saw most of its fighting on the western front.

"I hope so, for his family's sake. But on a more practical note, we do know his children and that is where we will have to search next, father or no father."

Still concerned now about Jeremy's welfare she asked, "Is there a way we can see if he lived to come home?"

"We can look into the medal records and there is an index for fallen WWI soldiers we can check. We can also see if there are any notices in the papers. Sometimes a paper would print the obituary of a local soldier who didn't make it back."

The August sun was bright, the sky was clear, and they were in need, of a break. "Come on, it's a beautiful day and we need some time away from the computer."

"My eyes *are* a little tired," she confessed.

"You can swim if you like, there aren't any rocks or lures to worry about around the dock." He laughed. "Grandad had some fishing line caught on his leg the first time he went swimming off the shore and right after that he took a rake and some scuba gear and got rid of anything that might endanger his grandkids."

Tessa thought of the prospect of floating in a warm refreshing lake. "I think I will."

He nodded in agreement. "Why don't you get changed and I'll fix us a belated lunch."

By the time Tessa had come back to the kitchen, attired in a modest one-piece, Wes had prepared sandwiches and drinks for their impromptu lunch.

He was balancing the food and juice bottles on a

circular tray.

"Let me help." She grabbed a plastic bottle as it was falling.

"Thanks, why don't you take the drinks down while I go and find some large towels."

They sat side by side on the dock beneath a radiant sun after their swim. Waves of puffy white clouds floated in slowly from the west dotting the blue. Tessa enjoyed their swim. They'd splashed water at each other, dove for shells, and raced to a diving platform set up next door. She hadn't realized how muscular Wes was. He was tall and straight of limb and his back muscles rippled as he swam, and she found herself watching him whenever he wasn't looking. They'd kissed and hugged, then kissed some more. Exhausted from swimming, they returned to their dock.

"Here." Wes passed Tessa a peanut butter sandwich.

Tessa pushed her wet hair back from her face and took a huge bite, then sighed in exaggerated bliss. "I didn't realize how hungry I was." She leaned back—her mouth full—and nodded her thanks at the opened bottle of pineapple juice Wes had placed on the arm of her chair. There was little breeze to disturb the water but enough to move the aspen leaves overhead, causing their silver undersides to glisten in the sunlight as they fluttered. Unlike the several birch trees, she noticed that the aspen trees were similar in colour but didn't appear to have peeling, paper-like bark, like the bark of the birch.

"This is nice, thank you," she said, and waved what was left of her sandwich, meant to encompass the whole lake experience.

Wes was happy that she appreciated their surroundings. He'd hoped she would be able to relax a bit even though thoughts of her research were always foremost on her mind. "You're welcome. Maybe after supper we can go for a canoe ride. Nan should be back tonight, unless her friend is worse."

There was a familiar sound of bells coming from the pocket of Tessa's swimsuit cover-up. She hesitated a moment before retrieving her phone, hoping it wasn't another call from her office. She nodded and smiled at Wes who was also hoping the subject of Keefer wouldn't arise again.

"Hi ... no, not yet. Maybe a couple of more days. How is he? Good, I'm glad they're enjoying him. I was more concerned if Tabs would enjoy toddlers. All right, I'll call you then. Bye."

"That was my sister. She has two young children who seem to have taken to Tabby. He seems to be adjusting to them all right too. As long as they don't pull his tail," she added with a smile. She leaned back in her chair and took the last bite of her sandwich. Before pressing the off button, Tessa noticed the message icon on her phone. "Oh, I didn't notice that before." She clicked that symbol and the corresponding message came up.

"Important?"

Wes watched as Tessa's face suddenly changed to one of concern.

"Yes. It's a message from Keefer," she said slowly, as if questioning how she had missed it before.

"What does it say?" Wes leaned over in his chair to get a better look as Tessa held out the phone. She read the message; her voice quiet as if reading a line etched on a long-lost tomb.

" 'Found something ... 1881 ... n—' " She'd suddenly grown pale as she stared back at the message. "It was sent the day he died." She shook her head, staring at the date. "That's strange ... do you think he had enough time to press send before he was hit, or maybe he was hit, dying, and sent it." A sudden sadness returned, thinking of her friend Keefer. Either way it didn't seem logical that a man texting then suddenly hit by a car would have the desire or ability to send the message.

Surely the phone would have been flung from his grip.

"Or, he didn't send it at all." suggested Wes. "I know we all do the pocket phone call on occasion by mistake, but I don't think you can send a pocket text. Then, it wouldn't have been sent by mistake." Tessa, agreed. Butt phoning someone from your cell phone when it accidentally rubbed the inside of your pants pocket was quite common, and annoying, but texting an actual message with correct spelling and then sending it seemed beyond the capability of every phone, smart or not.

"Okay, lets assume someone found his phone and sent the message Keefer had begun. Why would someone, do that?"

"Maybe someone saw what happened and found the phone and was just being kind, thinking it was important to his contact."

Tessa gave him a questionable look. "You don't really believe that?"

He smiled back to break the tension. "No. Would you do that? A normal person would give the phone to the police."

"True, unless the person was a dishonest person to begin with and wanted to keep the phone. That sort of person wouldn't talk to the police at all." She sat the phone down on the chair arm, thinking of the possible scenarios. "Okay, let's figure this out. Either it was Keefer or someone else. If it was Keefer before he was hit, he would have finished the message. If it was Keefer after he was hit, the police would have found the phone with him."

Wes took up the next possibility. "And if it was sent by someone else, the person either thought that the message was important for a friend or family member to see."

"Or ... they knew he was searching for info on Cyrus Griffin and wanted me to think Keefer had some proof and ... they want me to find it, so they can hide it later."

"That is a long shot, but possible." Another possible reason came to him. "Maybe they killed Keefer to get you to go public. I mean show up at his funeral, so they could stop you too. Remember, there's millions at stake." Wes leaned back in his chair, thinking, suddenly aware of the threat this posed to Tessa. "Well, there's one way to find out."

Wes reached toward the phone. "Do you mind?" Tessa nodded her approval and waited as Wes dialed. "Moose, it's Wes. Quick question. Did they find a cell phone with Keefer at the scene?" He tapped his fingers on the wooden arm, waiting. "Thanks."

He set the phone down again on the chair arm, then

114

looked at Tessa, a note of concern in his eyes. "They didn't find a phone with the body." He reached across and took her hand in his. "Let's assume because of the Hanley phone call, they know who you are and your connection with Keefer, but they don't know where you are, yet." Then a thought occurred to him. "Your phone should have GPS tracking ability which helps the 911 emergency people to locate you in time of trouble. It's probably best if you go into your settings and turn it off."

Tessa did as he suggested and felt a little safer for having done so.

Chapter 13

The thought that unscrupulous men were searching for her put a damper on their romantic swim. They finished up their lunch in silence, each with their own thoughts.

"Let's get back to work. I owe it to Keefer to get this done. And the more I feel threatened the more I know someone wants me to stop looking." Then a sudden thought caused a chill to run through her. "You don't think they would do something to my family?"

They stood in the kitchen now, their dirty dishes sitting on the counter. Tessa shivered in response to her revelation. "I don't think that would happen," said Wes softly. He put his arms around her and drew her to him. Lifting her chin, he kissed her gently. "I don't think they would go that far."

Tessa returned the hug, feeling now the muscles of his body, engulfing her, protecting her from danger. She felt safe in his arms. She looked up into his brown eyes, calm and reassuring. "What do you think Keefer's message meant?"

"It must have been important, obviously 1881 is the critical part of it and by that year it would seem it has something to do with Cyrus Griffin or Alexander Fenwick."

"That's what I had asked him to look into." She stepped

back so she could look into Wes's eyes. "But it's the 'n' that seems to be the important part. He'd started to write something because there is no period or ellipsis after it. I wonder what he was going to write?"

Wes sat in a wooden chair, one of four that edged the kitchen counter. Tessa joined him now at the counter. "It could mean November, that would fit in with the date," she offered.

"True ... what was the name of the guy Fairchild found as heir?" She leaned on Wes as she got up from her chair to hunt through her notes at the computer. The first few pages of her writing pad had that information.

"Here it is, Edmond Nolan, he lives in London."

Wes joined her at the computer table, and looked at the name, thinking. "If Keefer found something referring to Edmond Nolan, that could mean Fairchild's heir might be legit." He took his usual place at the table. "I'm sure we'll figure it out. Let's find Jeremy's kids."

They spent the next few hours sitting at the computer table, each looking into their separate genealogical sites. Tessa opened an account with The Genealogist, while Wes searched Find My Past.

Tessa had found the marriage first. Her excitement overshadowing her previous apprehension.

"Here it is, Sarah Fenwick married Mark Ainsley—printer—on February 23, 1926, in the Parish of St. George Hanover Square, London. She was eighteen and her father was written as Jeremy Fenwick-Occupation-Mercer." She repeated the occupation again, "What's a mercer?"

Wes leaned over to confirm the find. "I'm not sure." He turned back to his computer and Googled, 'Genealogical Occupations'. Several promising sites came up. He clicked on the first one then scrolled down to find the list of jobs beginning with the letter 'M'. "Here it is, Mercer: *A merchant of fine fabrics such as velvet.*"

"Good work, so we have a potential heir with this couple, if they had children. Let's keep looking for Harold and Emily."

After a few hours they both came to the same conclusion. The Fenwick family seemed to have disappeared. "Do you think they moved out of the country?"

"It's possible, he'd been a soldier and after the war, 1922 I think, they offered travel assistance and job opportunities to soldiers who emigrated to Australia and Canada. The colonies needed people and England had many people looking for work after the war."

"Go back to the marriage record again, check the

witnesses." He waited as the original image came into view. "Look there, her sister Emily is one of the witnesses."

"Maybe it was her mother, they both have the same name."

"True, but it does tell us the family were still in England as of February 1926, so it will help focus our search for them."

"So, we need to check outgoing ship records." She hesitated, before filling in the necessary particulars for 1926. "I've been thinking ... who is allowed, to contest a will? I mean, Hannah's father must have some relatives somewhere, cousins now, I guess. Here we are looking for her uncle's family on her grandfather's side: cousins ... second cousins. What about her grandfather's siblings? ... their descendants? Are they allowed to make a claim?"

"Well now ... there's a question. I think it depends what Hannah had specified in her will. I mean assuming she had a will which I can't imagine her lawyer ignoring. I do know, from many conversations with Tony, that if someone doesn't have a will, it opens up the possibility for relatives who might not be in a will to begin with, such as more distant relatives, especially if the person leaving the money, wasn't married and had no children." He smiled with a shrug. "So, let's hope

Hannah had a will and that she mentioned her uncle's family."

A thought occurred to Tessa. "I wonder if that's why her lawyer was upset. Hannah had mentioned he didn't like the idea she was looking into her grandfather's son."

"Could be, but all we can do is follow up on her wishes and let the courts decide."

"You're right, so we should start with 1926 and go forward. I'll start with the even years; you tackle the odd ones." On task again, Tessa was eager to find their family.

The sound of a car on the gravel lane-way interrupted their work. "Looks like Nan is back." He gave her arm a gentle squeeze. "I better go and help her in." Wes left his chair and went to help Nan with any possible groceries.

"I'll come too."

Tessa held the door open for Wes as he brought in the groceries Nan had purchased. Nan looked tired, her face pale and drawn. Tessa wondered how much sleep she'd had while away.

"I need to go back again tonight." she said, shrugging off her jacket and tossing it on to the living room couch.

"I'll make some tea," suggested Tessa.

"That would be most welcome, thank you."

Wes started taking groceries out of their canvas bags

and nodded his thanks as he found two bottles of wine among the food. He held up a bottle checking out the label. "These won't go to waste, thanks, Nan."

Tessa poured the boiling water into Nan's porcelain teapot. "How is your friend doing?"

"She went into the hospital last night. They think it's pneumonia." She poured some weak tea into the cup Tessa placed before her. "I'll have to go back and look after her pets. I knew there was little fresh food to eat for the two of you, so I stopped at the store first. I guess I could have brought them back with me, but I think they will feel more at ease if I stay in their home."

Nan sat at the counter; her cell phone laid before her. "Your phone is turned off again, isn't it?" She gave Wes a questionable gaze.

Wes smiled. "As usual, my dear Nan"

"Luckily mine was wasn't. Duffy called me. I guess he tried here first and when he couldn't get a hold of you, he called me."

"We were down by the lake for a while. We must have missed him."

She took a sip from her cup then set it down with a bit of a sigh. "I didn't know you were working for him."

"Well, technically I'm not. I'm researching a family for his employer." Wes put the last can into the pantry cupboard that hugged the far wall, hiding the concern showing now on his face. He made himself an instant coffee with the remainder of the hot water from the kettle and joined Tessa and Nan at the counter. "Did he mention why he wanted to speak with me?"

Tessa sat on a chair opposite Nan and wondered how much Nan knew about her grandson's job. She seemed unconcerned, which suggested to Tessa that she really had no idea what kind of work they were doing and didn't connect it directly to Duffy.

"No, just that when I saw you, to ask you to call him."

"I better call him now." He gave Tessa a knowing glance that suggested secrecy until he found out more.

The address and phone directory next to the wall phone was from the early seventies: the outer rectangular casing made of metal. Tony had drilled small holes in the back of the metal casing and screwed it to the wall, to make it easier for the caller to locate a number. Pressing a button along the bottom allowed the metal covering to pop open, revealing alphabetical tabs down the length of the right side. He quickly pressed the 'D' tab and a page with numerous telephone numbers and addresses for acquaintances whose name began with 'D' popped open. Many names had been crossed out over the years but there were two apparently still active.

"Duff, it's Wes." He turned and smiled reassuringly at Nan.

Tessa strained to listen to the phone conversation as she pretended to be interested in Nan's description of her friend's two pets. One was a white Cairn terrier and the other a black Scottie dog. "I'll head back in a couple of hours," she concluded.

Wes came back and took up his place at the counter. "I haven't spoken to Duffy for almost a year," said Nan, a little sorry for the lapse in time. "Was it important?"

"Duff's all right, but his house was broken into." He reached over and patted Nan's hand in reassurance. "Nothing to worry about. He's contacted the police already."

"Did they take anything? Does he need you to go there?" Tessa tried not to show her concern; there had to be more to it.

"No, I asked him. Nothing seems to be missing. I guess he came home, and the thief fled. He and the housekeeper had been shopping."

Nan pushed her empty cup toward the middle of the

counter as she got up. "That's good. I'm glad he's okay." She stifled a small yawn. "I think I'll have a wee nap before going back." She nodded at Tessa. "Thank you for thinking of the tea, dear," she said, then retired to her room for a well-deserved rest.

Chapter 14

Tessa waited until Nan had closed the bedroom door before whispering to Wes, "What actually happened?"

Wes motioned that they talk outside and led the way to the front porch. There was a slight breeze and the trees around the cottage made a soft swishing sound as the leaves brushed against the roof.

"He said they tore apart the library downstairs and they also searched Hannah's bedroom, and here's the strange bit, only the two rooms; nothing else."

Tessa leaned against the deck railing.
"Looking for something specific, that she might have put away in a safe place."

"Duff thinks he, or they, were looking for the copy of her will."

"That's right, a lawyer usually has one on file and the client usually gets a copy for their own records." Tessa turned toward Wes, trying to figure out the meaning of this. "So, if the lawyer wanted to destroy his copy of Hannah's will, then he would also have to have her copy destroyed as well. Which means the previous will would take effect."

She paused, thinking. "But if the lawyer said he found

an heir; doesn't that mean he also needs the last will to be read if he expects to introduce a long-lost relative as beneficiary. I mean if her previous will left money to her servants and charities, that would leave out any second or third cousin, wouldn't it?"

Wes rested his arms on the railing and nodded his head slightly. "I would have bet my last dime the lawyer was involved somehow, but as you say, it wouldn't make sense for him to destroy the will, not if he hoped to pass off a phony heir."

"Maybe it has something to do with Keefer and the message."

"Could be, let's try to find out."

The sun, now from the west, gave a welcome light that flooded the living room from the front window. Wes looked longingly at the blue sky reflected in the calm waters of the lake dotted with a few puffy clouds. He gave a quiet sigh and returned to his place at the computer table. There would be other days they could enjoy their surroundings more. He watched Tessa as she typed in her search. For the moment, he wished they had finished their work. He closed his eyes briefly and could feel her lips on his as they sat on the dock; there would be time for them later once they found Jeremy's family.

He worried most now for her safety and hoped the greed for millions didn't result in more deaths.

He gave her hand a pat as he waited for his screen to download his request. "You realize, checking into the distant past is easier than looking into the recent past? With various privacy laws it won't be easy." He glanced back at his screen hoping to find the name Fenwick on the list of passengers that had left English shores in 1927. There were two, but neither with the family names they were searching for.

"Here! 1926!" Tessa had been deep in thought as they worked side by side. She enlarged the page with the specific names she had found. "Look! Jeremy Fenwick, his wife Emily, son Harold and daughter Emily. They are on the steamer Letitia, destination Halifax, Nova Scotia, Canada! They're here!" She gave Wes a sideways hug in triumph, then enlarged the screen further to better read the categories at the top of the page.

"Jeremy Fenwick age forty-six, British, has never been to Canada before, passage paid by self and government. You were right: it seems he did get some government assistance." She followed the next two columns up checking for the headings, then read them aloud as Wes followed along. "If destined to a relative, friend or employer, state which and give full name and address. If not joining any person in Canada please give the address in Canada to which you are going." She scrolled back down to read the answers in that column which would hopefully give more information as to the family, and their final destination.

"I don't believe it, look!" she was excited now, as she pointed to the family's destination.

Wes leaned over and read aloud, "Step-brother- Mr. Harold Witherspoon, 83 Alcorn Ave, Toronto, Ontario. Only a couple of hours from here. Let's just hope they stayed in Ontario."

Next to that column listed the nearest relative: Sarah Ainsley, Waverley Terrace, Islington, London, England. "So, we have Sarah in England, and Harold and Emily in Ontario."

"We definitely need to find out what happened to them, and their children if they had any."

"Do you know what records are available for Ontario?"

Wes sat back and gave a faint sigh. "No. All of my research has been in Britain." He started to type. "But we can find out." He waited a moment as his search for 'available Ontario archive records' came up. "Here, birth records on line: 1869 to 1913; on line marriage registrations: 1869 to 1928, 1933 to 1936; and deaths: 1869 to roughly 1947 with a few missing years." He scrolled down. "This is interesting, they release records 104 years after registration unless needed for legal reasons."

"I'll take Family Search, you take Ancestry," he said.

"I'm starting to get overwhelmed again." Tessa sat back in her chair and looked up to the ceiling. "I need some grounding." She glanced at Wes and smiled.

He leaned over and turned her chin to face him and gave her a lengthy kiss. "Just what I needed too."

"Okay, start by looking for any Fenwicks in Ontario. Broaden the years to include the ones available."

"I'll go back into the British side and work on Sarah."

"What about Post Office Directories? Wouldn't they be available for years after 1925?"

He smiled at her suggestion. "Very good, hopefully, then we can narrow down where they were through the years."

An hour later the bedroom door opened, and Nan emerged looking a lot more rested than she had before. "Well, I'm off now." She went over to the storage bin by the fireplace and opened it, finding the few newspapers that it had held, gone.

"Do you need some papers, Nan?"

"I thought I'd take some with me, I'm not sure which

one of the dogs has a bladder problem but putting papers down might help with the clean up."

"I have a stack in my car that I scrounged from my neighbours recycle bins. I'll put some in your car."

"Thank you, Wes." She waited until she heard the back-door screen close with a bang. "I hope to be back tomorrow, but if I'm not I just wanted to tell you how pleased I was to have met you." She smiled warmly at Tessa. "Wes is a good lad."

Tessa felt herself flushing at this obvious approval of their perceived relationship. "We're really just colleagues," she attempted to explain, "but, I must admit, I do enjoy his company." Then smiled at the futility of trying to explain away her obvious attraction. Of course, they were more, than that. She could feel the chemistry between them from the start but for now that had to wait. Someone had died because of this endeavour: a friend, so she must focus now on finding out why.

"I put them in the trunk, Nan." Wes gave her a hug farewell. "Do drive safely,"—then he pulled his cell phone out of his jeans pocket— "and I promise to keep my phone on ... just in case."

She gave Wes a slight pat on his arm in passing. "See

you tomorrow or the next day." And she was gone.

Wes joined Tessa at the computer table. "Well at least we have more than hotdogs for supper tonight."

"I like your Nan. You do realize that she thinks we're a couple."

"Yes, she expressed that to me earlier. I didn't want her to know the real reason for our work and then worry about it later. She was already upset with Duffy's news." Then something close to shock crossed his face. "You mean she asked you?"

Tessa smiled at his discomfiture. "No, she just implied that she was fine with it."

"What did you say?" he asked, keeping his eyes on his screen.

"I said that I enjoyed your company, and we were colleagues working on an important job."

His brows raised in contemplation. "You do? I mean ... enjoy my company?"

"Yes ... here." She reached over and drew him to her and gave him a sensuous kiss. "Now back to work."

The awkwardness passed, the two settled into their searching.

"Okay, I've found Sarah's first child, a boy named

Jeremy, after his grandfather, born in 1928, Islington, London." He sat back in triumph. "Heir number one!" He checked the next five years and found no other civil registration record stating another child. Then he found the reason. Sarah had apparently died in child birth the same month as her child was born. He had begun to feel for this family and felt saddened with the results he'd found. Sarah's husband had remarried a year later, and the child seemed to have survived after his mother's death. Wes made careful notes for each: noting location, year, months, volume and page numbers, all of which would be needed later to order corresponding certificates. Then he added Jeremy Ainsley as a potential heir to his list of names.

"How are you doing?" He leaned over and checked her note pad for written results then noticed a new website she had jotted down. "What's this one?"

"This is a fantastic site I just found by accident." Tessa closed the window she was viewing and opened a new window up with the search screen beckoning a topic. "I just searched for Toronto directories and came up with this one from the Toronto Library." She scrolled through the page, demonstrating this new resource. "I'm not sure what a Might directory means, but it has all the years we're looking for and I think I found Jeremy Fenwick." She went back to the page she had saved—

1928 and scrolled down the list of names beginning with the letter 'F'. "Here, Jeremy Fenwick, slsmn—which I think means salesman—Simpsons, 87 Alcorn Ave." Excited now with her find she showed Wes her notes on Harold Witherspoon who live on the same street a few doors away.

"I'd say you've lucked out with this one, and with his stepbrother nearby it's almost a certainty. See how far you can trace him and, also check on his son." The sun was at the far side of the lake, low in the sky now and shining into the cottage from the large picture window. Wes made a note in his book in reference to the page he had been working on, then leaned back with a sigh. "I'm getting a little hungry. What about breaking for a …," he said, checking his watch, "early supper?"

Tessa smiled at him, a small rumble from her stomach reminding her they hadn't eaten since their snack at the dock. "I was hoping you would suggest that. I'll save my work then join you."

It wasn't long before Wes was in the kitchen searching the pantry for suitable items. "Nan, is a dear," he said softly, "she's thought of everything." He picked up a package of spaghetti. "We've had a lot of meat the last two days, how about spaghetti and salad?"

"Sounds good. Why don't I get the salad going and you can take care of the sauce and spaghetti?" He looked at the cans of prepared pasta sauce Nan had purchased and contemplated the job of cleaning and preparing lettuce to stirring pasta and opening a can of sauce. "That I can do."

Tessa had the pot of water already on the stove. She added a teaspoon full of salt then gave her hand a wave implying it was all his. Wes opened the plastic package of spaghetti. Behind the cans of sauce, he found the plastic device Nan used for measuring out portions. He laid the appropriate amount in the two-portion section, then carefully cracked the spaghetti in half ready for the pot. He noticed Tessa watching him from the sink as she rinsed the romaine, then added another single portion to the pile. "A little extra for our Herbert," he said softly, as if embarrassed by the kind gesture.

"Herbert?"

"The skunk. Nan named him after her Uncle Herbert."

Tessa tore the last of the romaine lettuce into pieces before surmising the reason for this association. "Because he smelled?"

Wes gave a snort of laughter at her reasoning. "No,

because he liked to wear black suits and just happened to have a white streak of hair that went from his forehead along his part line.

"Oh." Tessa chuckled at the visual image this placed in her mind. "Herbert will be pleased, I'm sure." Tessa went to the fridge for the Caesar salad-dressing and gave Wes a warm hug from behind on passing. She glanced at the boiling water. "How's the spaghetti coming along?"

"Almost done." He reached into the boiling water with a fork and captured one strand to test, "Another two minutes."

"Why don't we eat on the deck?" he suggested. "I'll keep Herbert's for after dark."

Chapter 15

At one end of the porch, Nan had arranged a bistro table with matching chairs so that a clear view of the lake could be seen.

They sat quietly, enjoying the lake; the soft sound of the waves as they meandered toward the shore, the slight rustle of the leaves in the trees, a chipmunk as it made a deep chirp sound to his friends. A loon across from them, on the west side of the lake gave a haunting call and was answered moments later by another further up the lake. A canoe hugging the shore line went slowly by as its occupant waved a greeting.

A squirrel sitting in a tree to the side of the deck raised his voice in protest as a large bird began drilling in the trunk above his branch intent on finding insects.

"What kind of woodpecker is that?" she asked, noticing the unique look of a bird she had never seen before. The only woodpeckers she had seen in her yard were the small black and white downy woodpeckers that came for the suet she hung out during the winter.

Wes had seen the bird light on the branch, then move to drum on the tree trunk and nodded. "It's a pilated woodpecker, beautiful, isn't he? I think he's one of the largest woodpeckers." He watched as the bird moved around the tree pecking into the bark at various spots. "This one has been around for a few years now."

"He looks a lot like Woody Woodpecker, doesn't he?" She smiled remembering the annoying cartoon character. Oblivious to the squirrel's chattering the woodpecker continued his drilling, then flew off after Tessa moved her metal chair along the wooden deck to get up. "Oh, I didn't mean to frighten him, I just wanted to get some peanuts for the squirrel."

"Nan keeps a jar just inside the door."

She brought back five and placed them at strategic spots along the railing, so they could better see the small animal from their table. He climbed the deck at a safe distance and took the peanut that posed the least danger, then sat eating his prize.

Their meal finished, they sat silently, each with their own thoughts. She'd known this man only for a few days and yet some how they were now connected. In those few days she found him to be kind, caring and to her surprise, a bit shy. He wasn't like some others she'd dated that as soon as the opportunity offered, had wandering hands all over her. Wes was a professional like herself, which didn't mean he wasn't like most guys, but he respected her and what she was doing and wanted to be a part of that.

They had worked continuously, at looking for Hannah's lost family and she admired his expertise and resolve. All that aside, he was also a very attractive man and if she was being honest with herself, she found him so, and enjoyed the attention—however reserved—he was paying her. He was a partner she enjoyed working with, and hoped maybe later when this was over, they could continue a more personal relationship.

Wes broke the silence. "Lucky guy, no blue jays around today to steal his meal." The small squirrel lay prone on his branch now, his legs sprawled out on either side.

His thoughts had turned more to their search and to their safety in what might be a dangerous endeavour. "Is there some way you could give your sister the cottage phone number … in some sort of code in case she needs to communicate with you?"

Tessa considered this for a moment wondering why Wes had suggested such a thing. "Do you think she might be in some sort of danger?"

"No, not directly, but she is checking up on your home isn't she?"

"Yes."

"Maybe we need a safe way for her to communicate with you ... just in case," he added, not wanting to alarm her further. If Tessa wasn't at Keefer's funeral in the next few days, they, whoever 'they' were, might try other ways of finding out where she was.

Tessa nodded in agreement. "Better play it safe, seeing we don't know what we're up against. Give me a few minutes to figure something out." Wes went back inside to find some paper for her to write on.

After figuring out a code that only the two sisters would know, Tessa was ready to call her sister using Wes's cell phone.

"Hi, it's me ... yes. Get a pen and paper ... okay," she looked anxiously at Wes, hoping her sister wouldn't ask too many questions while she tried to relay her information in less than a minute.

"I'm going to give you a phone number in code. Without saying anything, write this down. Tabby's age times ninety, minus Mom's birthday. Next part, our old house number minus Terry's age. And the last part: Dad's birth year plus eighty-four. You can reach me at this number, but don't use your phone. Use a friend's phone or a neighbours' or pick up a burner phone. Call me any day at ten in the morning or ten at night, only if there is any problem."

"No. I'm fine. I'm working on something important. I just need to stay where I am for a few more days without anyone knowing, not even the people at work … oh, and don't go over to my house.

"Okay, love you. Give Tabs a kiss for me." She rushed this last bit, as Wes signaled that she was approaching a minute. To talk longer might be dangerous if others were listening in and trying to trace the call.

"Well done. Let's hope no one has looked for a connection between you two yet." How many were there, he wondered? Surely the lawyer had his own detectives now. Would they connect him with Duffy or Nan? The only way they could find her was through her phone. Thinking she would go to Keefer's funeral; would they consider trying to trace her cell phone or just wait until she showed up? Was that why Hanley had called her? No, he was confident they were safe here, but he would be cautious just the same. "Did she sound upset?"

"A little, but I think letting her know she can call was reassuring. She'll be careful, after all she knows what kind of job I have. I think she actually enjoys the intrigue of it all."

"Speaking of job, why don't you go back to the

Toronto directories you found while I quickly clean up."

When Wes joined her at the table, Tessa had already found Jeremy living at the same address with the same job for the years 1928 through to 1930. Harold was now Harry in the directory and appeared at the same address obviously living at home and working as a clerk's assistant. It was the beginning of the Great Depression and Tessa wondered if any of them would be keeping their jobs as the years passed.

He watched her covertly as his computer warmed up distracting him for a moment. She was beautiful, determined and he enjoyed their time together, sharing in her discoveries. "You know I think we are doing quite well, considering. We've found Jeremy Fenwick aka Griffin and his family. So now we just have to follow his children in the records. Hopefully we will find his grandchildren here in Canada."

"Well, not so fast. I've lost Harry at 1940. His father is still living in Toronto but no mention of a Harold or Harry Fenwick." She flipped through the pages of her notes double checking the dates. "Do you think he joined the Army?"

"That's possible but as far as I know, the only on-line records available are for the soldiers who died during WWII. I don't know where to look for general enlistees, if there are any, considering privacy laws."

Tessa folded her note pad with a fatalistic sigh, "Yeah, privacy issues again." Then a thought occurred. "Why would the government honour the dead but not let us know the names of the heroes who were in the war and survived. That doesn't seem fair."

"True, and you would think, some, if not all the regiments have lists of their men. It would seem easier if there was a complete list, though."

"How far do the Toronto directories go?"

"I did see one for 1969 but I haven't checked it yet. I got as far as the 1951 directory. Jeremy was still alive but retired. And still no listing for Harold."

"I suppose he could have moved to another area in Canada. You said you looked in the directories right after the war?" Tessa nodded. "Usually a soldier would return home, but I think we should check to see if he married and stayed in England, or perhaps he was killed in the war. Once we check that with no results, we'll have to widen our search to all of Canada or check the British directories; maybe he returned to England and decided to stay." He opened a page where he had listed the Canadian records available, then nodded as he read the availability of the death records. "Okay, we can check on line for the years 1939-1947. But remember absence doesn't mean proof. He may have had a car accident in 1948. All we can do now is rule out what we are able to look at on-line."

"All right." Tessa turned to a digital image page she had been working on. "Here, I made a new chart for Jeremy's family, just to keep the children straight." She scrolled down to three younger Fenwicks. "Do you have their birth dates handy?"

Wes turned to the notes he had made. "Yes, and I have Sarah's son as well."

Tessa copied down the dates then finalized her page. "So, we have three people to find: Jeremy Ainsley, Emily Fenwick and Harold Fenwick."

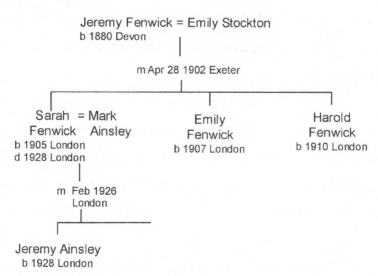

Wes jotted down a note before agreeing. "You know,

Harold was British, maybe he joined the British Military, or maybe he simply went back and later died there. I think I'll check the deaths first. I believe their death index goes to 2005."

The sun was just above the tree line at the west side of the lake, causing dark shadows along the shore. The sky gave a faint tint of pink to the underside of the few clouds that crowded the horizon.

Tessa felt the table move then heard Wes give a faint, "Oh …"

"What did you find?" She leaned over thinking Wes had found their missing Harold Fenwick.

"What month did the family move to Canada?"

Tessa flipped back through her notes. "May of 1926, why?"

"I found a death for an Emily Fenwick age nineteen." Tessa leaned over to get a better look as Wes enlarged the entry. It was the right year and the right quarter. Births marriages and deaths were listed under one of four quarters of the year, and this record showed this Emily had died in the April to June quarter of the year.

"It seems because the ship was a British ship the death was recorded under British Civil Registration, which to me implies she died at sea, although that has to be proven."

Tessa was quiet for a moment. "That's sad, I wonder what she died of? Would they have buried her at sea in 1926?"

Wes shook his head slowly, and he shrugged slightly. "I suppose the certificate or ship records might say, but that's something we can figure out later if we need to. Now we have two possible heirs left—Harry Fenwick and Jeremy Ainsley."

By ten o'clock the two sat next to each other at the back door in darkness, quietly awaiting the arrival of Herbert the skunk. They'd fixed themselves a late snack of veggies, cheese and crackers for the event and now sat with an accompanying glass of wine as they watched. "Look! There!"

Wes followed her gaze to the woodpile that lined the edge of the property. "I don't think so."

It was nothing, just a shadow that moved as a tree branch swayed. The moon had come out now and gave an eerie glow to familiar things. Wes leaned over and whispered into her ear. "He's under my vehicle." Right where they had left the last snack, the skunk had returned for this second feast and like before he used his paw to pull the aluminum tray into the darkness before eating.

"I'm glad he found it, but since we can't watch him now in the dark, we might as well go and enjoy our meal in front of the fire."

Tessa agreed and took his glass while Wes gathered up their plates and boxes of crackers, as Tessa led the way. He placed their snack on the impromptu table by the fireplace and then checked the wood box.

"This shouldn't take long."

The lake was dark now, the moon obviously covered by a wave of cloud. The only thing visible from the large picture window was the railing and a few close trees whose ghostly image took form from the reflected light within the cottage.

Wes was choosing the kindling wood from the left side of the window seat storage, then went to the right side to retrieve a few sheets of newspaper. "I'm glad I brought a larger stash of newspapers. I'll have to remind Tony to bring extra next time he comes up." He crumpled the sheets of newsprint into a ball then placed the kindling teepee-style over the paper.

Tessa watched as the flames took hold and the newspaper burned to a flakey char. "Newspapers," she said softly as her mind caught on to her idea. "Wes, do you think Keefer was trying to tell us he found something in an 1881 newspaper?"

Wes stopped as he was about to add a larger chunk of wood to the small blaze, then turned slowly with the wood still in his hand. A smile spread across his face. "It's very possible, and newspaper records do exist."

Excited now at the thought of a new clue, Tessa was eager to pursue this last message sent by Keefer. "And if we're talking about 1881, it probably has something to do with Alexander Fenwick or Cyrus Griffin." Tessa brought his glass of wine over to him then sat on the couch before the fireplace.

"Are they on line?"

Wes took his glass of wine after adding new logs to his fire, then sat next to her.

"There is a newspaper site. I've seen it mentioned on other sites as I've worked on my own family."

"Maybe we will find a connection between Alexander and Cyrus somehow."

He pulled the TV tray closer. "It's our only lead so let's follow it." He picked up a piece of cheddar cheese then chose an herbal cracker to go with it. "So, tomorrow we will look for a newspaper site and you can look there while I take over hunting for Harry Fenwick and Jeremy Ainsley."

They clinked their wine glasses in a silent toast.

Chapter 16

Morning found the sun pouring into Tessa's window. From the angle of the rays coming through the trees, it appeared to be mid-morning. It was late, and Wes was up already. She could hear the sound of an axe in the back yard, as it split the foot-length size of logs—that had been stacked in a neat row along the drive by his brother Tony—into smaller sizes that Nan could comfortably carry. Pine, which would burn easier and faster, was chopped into smaller pieces which were placed in a separate bin to be used as kindling.

The sun was bright this morning and filled her with renewed hope. They had talked about this last night until well past midnight: how they were going to approach today's work. She had lain in her bed thinking about Keefer and his last message: did it mean newspaper? Given the context—what else could it mean? It was well into early morning before she had fallen asleep, her mind racing with various scenarios. But now—she checked the clock—at 9:05 in the morning she was awake and ready to work, and from the sound of it, so was Wes.

She slipped into her housecoat then slid the window open. "Good morning. What would you like for breakfast?"

He stopped and rested the axe blade on the stump he was using for splitting the kindling wood. The morning was warm already, and he'd taken his shirt off, his body sweaty with the exertion. He wiped a hand across his forehead, sweeping his hair from his eyes, before answering. "Boiled eggs…three minutes with toast and bacon?"

"Can do … twenty minutes?"

"Perfect, I should be finished by then."

The chopping renewed as Tessa dressed. It would be a busy day. She had had little sleep, her mind unable to rest, now that she felt they had figured out Keefer's message. There was a good chance they might be wrong, but she would spend time searching until all avenues had been checked. If Keefer had found something, she was confident they could find it too, and hopefully prove some connection between Alexander and Cyrus.

Finding the necessary food items and cooking utensils, Tessa had breakfast for the two of them ready as Wes appeared from the bathroom after a quick shower. They sat together at the counter, each deep within their own thoughts. "It's amazing how much thinking goes on during physical labour." He took another bit of the crispy bacon from his plate. "Your body is doing the physical task, but your mind just goes off on its own thoughts. I couldn't help feel but energized by the work we've done so far."

"I know. I think we'll find the link between the two families. I just hope it's today."

Wes picked up a one of his toasted soldiers and dipped it into the second soft-boiled egg. He looked at her as he raised the eggy toast. "Interesting how you cut the toast into strips, my mum used to do that for me too." He smiled at the thought, then finished the remainder of his eggs and toast.

"I'd like to tackle the newspaper clue, if you don't mind continuing the search for the kids."

"That's fine. We should find a good British newspaper site, then subscribe. I'll follow through with the sites we've been using to try to track the kids." He took a swallow of his coffee to wash the remaining breakfast down. "I'm sure you have your sources as I have mine, so when we start to get close to the present-day, we may have to call upon those people to track any potential descendants."

Tessa agreed, and mentally started thinking of whom she could call upon to help her with the search. A moment of sadness came over her as she thought of Keefer. It was his funeral today—she'd seen the notice on the internet—and she wondered if the church service was over now, and she could envision the mourners making their way in convoy to the cemetery. She felt sorrow at not being there but felt too she could better serve his memory by finding out what he had died for.

"Why don't I clean up and you go on ahead and start looking for Jeremy's people."

Wes picked up the last piece of bacon and headed over to the computer table, taking his topped-up coffee mug with him. By the time Tessa had joined him he had begun to download a page referring to Canadian soldiers who had died in WWII. She sat next to him, her hand resting on his as the page came up. "What site is this?"

"Well, I started out at Veterans Affairs, then, I found that there is a Second World War Book of Remembrance that lists the names of the war dead, which also led me to The Canadian Virtual War Memorial. They have a list of the Canadian soldiers who died in WWII, which shows their branch, their age, where they died and various other information; if family added more personal facts about the soldier. They even have a Book of Remembrance for the soldiers in the Boer War, amazing. They sat quietly, hoping not to find the name of Harold Fenwick among the soldiers who had perished. "There." Tessa watched as Wes opened-up the page of the first of five Harold/Harry Fenwicks. A young man who had died in France. He had been nineteen at the time of his death; and had joined the Army in Calgary—not theirs.

The next two had birth years close to their Harry and had joined the armed forces in Ontario. One the Airforce and the other the Army. Both had died in France and both were buried there as well.

"I wonder if either of these are our Harry Fenwick?" Tessa had asked as the first screen came up.

The first of these had joined the Airforce, and they had scanned the information, hoping for something that would confirm or deny that he was their Harry Fenwick. "No. Look here under Additional Information: the parents names are different." He had pointed out the section that included more personal information.

The next Harold Fenwick had joined the Army. He had been nearly the same age as the man they hunted and had died in 1945. Unlike the Airforce Fenwick there was no additional information to show—whether, or not—he was Jeremy's son. "This might be him. Let's check the next one."

Wes opened-up the fourth name, enlarging the screen. "Oh ..." He read aloud the information for this Harold Fenwick. "Age thirty-three. Army, Royal Canadian Corps of

Signals. Died December 15,1944. Buried in the Netherlands." He moved the screen to the right to include the Additional Information section. Son of William and Clara Fenwick of Toronto. Husband of Grace Fenwick of Hamilton. "Close ... I was hoping it wouldn't be him." He returned to the page of results and opened the information for the last Harry Fenwick.

Tessa had a sinking feeling as she glanced quickly at the death information for this soldier.

"Harry Fenwick," Wes began, "Age thirty-two. Army, Queens Own Rifles of Canada. Died July 7, 1944. Buried; Calvados, France." He moved the screen over to the right where the more personal information could be listed. A chill went down Tessa's arms as Wes read the words. "Son of Jeremy and Emily Fenwick of Toronto."

Following the page down they saw a news article describing his loss to the community with a picture of the deceased soldier.

Both were quiet for a few moments, each feeling the loss for a family they didn't know. Their research had followed this family through the years, and now they had become close enough to feel a sadness for them.

"Okay, I guess that's that. We'll have to get the actual certificates for Harry and Emily and Sarah. That leaves just

Sarah's son, Jeremy Ainsley."

"But maybe Harry had a family"

"I don't think so. The family surely would have added that when they added his parents' names."

He gave Tessa's hand a warm squeeze. "Let's work until lunch time, then take a break. I'll start looking for Jeremy Ainsley and you follow up on Keefer's clue."

"Okay. Where is the information for the newspaper site?" She leaned closer to see the notes Wes had made about the new web site they had subscribed to—Newspapers.com. He took her face in his hands and gave her a lengthy kiss. "That should hold you over till lunch." He smiled as her face lost its seriousness."

Chapter 17

It was just after two o'clock and they had sat side by side barely talking, as each followed their respective searches.

Tessa had started looking into the 1881 Devon newspapers, looking for anything to do with Alexander Fenwick or Cyrus Griffin. She'd gone through the whole year, but with no luck and now leaned back in her chair with a sigh. "How are you doing?"

"Well, I started by looking for Jeremy's father, Mark Ainsley. He was on the 1939 Register, so I checked for a death and found that he died in 1949. Then I started to wonder about Jeremy himself. I checked for his name in the marriage and deaths records in England for the years after the war; and didn't find him."

"I know the British Government had an evacuee plan figured out before the war for children, so I wondered if he had been sent abroad when the war started? He would have been ten or eleven, in 1939. And as I didn't find his name in the British records, he either died, or stayed where he was after the war." He leaned back, suggesting her opinion on this train of thought.

"It sounds like a reasonable deduction. So where do

you look?"

"I guess I'll have to check the statistics for Australia, Canada and the United States and see if I can find a Jeremy Fenwick that matches …" he paused, "then, see if any of the child evacuee ships were sunk. That might be a reason he hasn't shown up." He shook his head in frustration at the long search ahead.

"Come on, let's break for lunch," she said. "I saw some tuna in the cupboard. What about toasted, tuna salad sandwiches. We have some lettuce left too."

They sat in comparable silence at the bistro table on the front deck, each with their thoughts. They had found the children of Jeremy Fenwick and the only possible person left that could inherit Hannah's fortune was Sarah's son Jeremy Ainsley. This was the first time Tessa had seen Wes's spirits fade during their hunt. She could understand how he felt. He had hoped Harry Fenwick had prospered and lived a long life after the war, if only for the sake of his parents who had already lost two children. Did Jeremy and Emily know about their grandson? Did they offer to care for him after his mother's death? Had he come to them for safety before the war? All questions that would be eventually answered, she hoped.

And what of Cyrus Griffin during these years? He had lived a privileged life for years after 1881. And how did Alexander become Cyrus Griffin? This was a question she hoped would be answered once she found out what Keefer's message meant.

She finished the last of her sandwich, then washed it down with the last of her juice. "There's more juice in the cupboard," offered Wes.

"No, thanks." She tided her dishes. "I was just wondering where to go from here. I checked the whole year in the newspapers for Devon … and … nothing."

Drawn out of his mood by Tessa's lack of results, he thought seriously as to how to proceed. "Well, the last place we found Alexander Fenwick was on the '81 census, and we know what happened to his kids." He paused, thinking. "There was another person living with them … his wife's brother. What was his name?"

"James Tyrell."

"You mentioned he was a mariner. What if Alexander had some tie with him, to the sea I mean. Maybe try the lateral route again and look for James Tyrell. And if Tyrell is found somewhere with Cyrus Griffin, he might be the connection we need to tie Alexander and Cyrus together."

His spirits renewed by this sudden revelation, he picked up their dishes and empty bottles. There was a breeze from the lake that beckoned them, the sun hiding sporadically behind fluffy clouds. It was a beautiful day, tempting them, but they had work to do.

They had gone back to their work after their lunch break, hopeful, yet concerned that maybe this was all for nothing. Wes had started with Australia then moved on to the United States. He had found one evacuee ship that had been torpedoed while trying to reach Canada. "This site …" he switched back to the home page of a new site that outlined almost everything about the evacuees' plight—except names. "Here, this site has tons of information about, WWII British Child Evacuees to Canada. It mentions some ships that they came on. And I did find one ship that was sunk by German torpedoes, which sort of ended the program because people were so upset about it, Churchill had no choice. It did say that over 5,000 children came to Canada under other arrangements, like relatives or friends while 1,500 came under government supervision."

What I didn't realize is that some also went to South Africa and New Zealand. What I didn't realize too, is that many religious organizations and service clubs sponsored children." He tossed his pen on the table. "It's frustrating. Many genealogical sites claim they have passenger list records, and yet when I go to search them, they conveniently leave out the war years. I don't know why that would be when there are records for after the war and before?"

Tessa had stopped her work and listened as Wes vent his frustration. "I guess, then, he could be anywhere, if he lived." She glanced at the notes he had made in silence as he had read the pages of this new site.

"Well, there is some good news. I checked the National Archives of Britain and found that individual records will only be open if the person is now deceased, but there are no lists or registers of evacuees available online, which implies that they can be searched somewhere else. They did however explain how to go about searching on a genealogical site for the '39 register. I did that, and I did find a J. Ainsley, which matched the birth year, living with his father. I viewed the transcript and saw under occupation it said, 'at school evacuees.' Then I went to view the actual page and his name was blackened out and said, 'this record is officially closed.'

"Doesn't that mean he could still be alive?" Tessa grabbed her pencil and did a quick calculation. "Wes! He'd be ninety now."

159

"We can check for deaths, but marriage seems to intrude on privacy laws. But I can't even narrow down what continent he might be on, let alone what country."

"Well, let's start with the obvious. We know his father knew Sarah's parents and may have known they came to Canada. I think we should start looking in Canada, assuming the father didn't also have friends or family somewhere else. You said you found some ships that came to Halifax. Maybe we can look them up and see if there is more information."

"There was something on the site I was looking at." Wes flipped a page of his note pad and reloaded the page he had been reading. He scrolled down until he came to the description of the ships. "Here, the Hilary and the Anselm. And I think with the number of evacuees that were sent to Canada it might be a good place to start our search. If we find nothing, then Australia would be the next choice."

"I think it's time to call in our own detectives, now that there is a chance, he still might be alive, and possibly have descendants," suggested Tessa. "I have two people in Toronto, Chelsey and Earl, who can start searching the public records for divorce, marriage, voter lists and criminal records. And Neal lives in Hamilton, his specialty is the military."

"And I have Mike in Kingston, who can check out

electoral records and go to Ottawa and search records there, and of course Moose in Toronto. Let's just hope Jeremy Ainsley wasn't sent to the U.S., New Zealand or Australia instead."

"So, you contact yours and I'll contact mine. We'll use my phone." He gave her hand a pat in finality. "Then, we go down to the lake and have a break."

Early evening found the two at the edge of the lake taking advantage of the still warm sun. Tessa wanted to continue looking into Keefer's clue and now that they would pass on their information to other colleagues, whose job it was to find people in the 21st century, she felt enthusiastic that she and Wes would continue to look for the meaning of '1881 ... n'.

Wes had suggested a canoe ride before supper and the two had headed up the length of the lake, Tessa seated in the bottom as she leaned against the thwart in front of the seat Wes was sitting on. He paddled slowly along the shoreline stopping now and then to kiss her under the shade of a bending tree, their faces hidden by its branches. "I'm glad you're here," he'd said, softly, to her again.

Tessa had replied in kind and reflected that she was indeed glad that she had met Wes and was spending this time with him.

He moved the branch away with his paddle as they resumed their ride. "Do you suppose we can continue to see each other after we're finished here?"

Tessa smiled. "I don't know why not? your Nan seems to think it's okay." She turned her face toward his inviting another kiss which he promptly gave. "Besides, I'm starting to get use to you being around."

Wes gave a dutiful grin back. "Good," he said, then continued paddling.

Tessa's mind had switched back to their job. "Do you think we'll hear something soon?"

"Maybe, it depends if they have the time to help us right away. My people work for others besides me, but I did say it was urgent."

"I suppose we could start using the phone directory or the internet, if we don't get any results right away from them. It's not as if Ainsley is a common name." The water was warm as the air started to cool and Tessa trailed her hand along the surface causing a small ripple as they moved. "Although, that may take quite a while."

"You know, I had a friend who almost lost his finger doing that." He nodded, indicating her hand trailing in the water."

She gave her hand a quick jerk out of the water then smiled suspiciously, wondering if Wes was just teasing her. "Well, we don't have piranha fish in Canada, so how did that happen?"

"He was sitting sideways across the canoe with his buddy on the other side facing him, and both had their hands in the water. A fish came up and took hold thinking the fingers were food." He tried to keep a straight face as she followed along with his story. "Luckily for him it was a bass and not a big pike with sharp teeth."

Tessa had second thoughts about keeping her fingers in the water and removed her hand discretely, as Wes laughed at her reaction.

"Would you like to pull up on shore somewhere and eat?" They'd brought a thermal picnic bag with a small snack to hold them over until they got back.

Tessa sat up and looked around. There were two islands close together further up the lake, one smaller than the other but each covered with scraggly pines, brush and rocks. Wes docked their canoe on the larger of the two, then pulled the front up so it was well secured by the sandy bottom of the shore. He held Tessa's hand as she stepped out onto a flattened rock that jutted out into the water. Tessa had prepared the sandwiches while he had called his contacts and he had unearthed the canoe from the side of the cottage as she had called hers. Now they sat together on an old beach blanket Wes had thought to bring at the last minute, sharing peanut butter sandwiches and soda.

Their spot faced south but they could see the sun as it sank closer to the treed horizon. A seagull spotted the two and swooped down to investigate. He landed on the rock by the canoe then shook his wings in an outward fluff before making a trumpeting screech. He plopped into the water then slowly came closer, apparently interested in anything that appeared to be food. He dipped his head several times in a fruitless gesture, hoping to get noticed. "Don't give him anything just yet," warned Wes. "His friends will be all over this island if they know there's food around."

"Well, I must admit he's being very polite, so far,"— she tore off a piece of crust from the last of her sandwich and folded it back in the plastic wrap— "so, I'll save this for him."

To their right a small motor boat with an older gentleman running the motor, left his dock and headed toward the general store. The sun was sinking and made the few clouds in the sky, a soft shade of purple. "You like it up here, don't you?" she asked.

"What's not to like. It's quiet, I can work in peace, and enjoy the water and the surrounding forest while I'm doing it." He took her hand in his. "What about you?" he asked.

Tessa finished her soda before answering, "I think I would be interested in seeing if there are any cottages for sale here. I wouldn't always have to be in the city to work, and as you say it is relaxing." Finished their sandwiches, Tessa unwrapped her scrap of crust.

Wes had saved some of his too. "Let's hope he likes peanut butter."

Chapter 18

It was late summer, and the evenings were starting to become chilly. They sat comfortably on the shore, before a generous fire watching the lake as the few people still up on vacation spent the last hours of twilight, boating or fishing. "Dan's caught a big one, I can hear him calling to his wife on the beach." They watched as neighbour Dan hauled in a nice-sized fish, cheering in delight.

They had augmented their earlier sandwich with roasted hotdogs over the fire and now sat, each with a glass of wine, enjoying the last of the day.

The last of the sun finally faded from view leaving the sky a deep, velvet blue. The first star of the night appeared and the two sat back in their chairs watching the night sky. Tessa closed her eyes and made a wish, then smiled as Wes tried to get her to tell what it was.

There was a rustling close by in the small shrubs that lined the shore on either side of the dock. "I hope that's not Herbert," she said, feigning fear of being sprayed by a disgruntled skunk.

Wes enjoyed the companionship they shared. His initial protective feelings for Tessa had advanced to more romantic ones. He realized too, that here, she was vulnerable, and took pains not to be too forward. He wanted her to like him for his own sake, and not because of their close work situation and isolation. He wanted nothing more than to take her in his arms and make love to her this moment, but knew too, to try was to possibly lose her and he wouldn't chance that. So, he would bide his time and when this was all over, and her work was done, he would court her properly—and win her.

The almost, full moon shone, its light reflecting off the lakewater before them. It was peaceful with only the sound of fisherman Dan as he rowed back towards his dock. The water lapped peacefully against the dock's wooden structure. A loon further up the lake gave its haunting, lonely cry.

"I wonder …" Tessa was interrupted by the faint ring of the kitchen phone. Wes jumped up; half startled by the ringing as well as eagerness to get to the phone before the person hung up.

Wes took the earthen, carved steps two at a time, as Tessa followed. It was nearly ten o'clock and a sudden urgency came over her as she anticipated her sister's call.

"Hello. Hi …" Out of breath, he waited as the person on the other end expressed the reason for their call. "She's here …" He glanced at Tessa who was watching him, intently.

"Your sister."

Tessa took the proffered kitchen phone. "Hi, Sis."

She listened as her sister explained her call. She had received news from Mary, Tessa's neighbour, that Tessa's house had been broken into. The police arrived shortly after Mary called and had determined that the thief had entered through a side window. He had apparently left the exposed electronics—computer, television, sound system—and had rummaged through drawers and cupboards instead, apparently looking for drugs or cash. Mary wasn't sure if anything of value had been taken but after the police secured the property, she had locked up the home again and called Tessa's sister.

Wes's face was blank as he watched Tessa, able to hear the muffled sound of her sister's voice. "No, don't go over. I'll take care of it from here. Okay, bye." Tessa was shaken, uncertain what to do now. She came back to a worried Wes and sat opposite him at the counter.

"My house was broken into. She said the police made sure the place was secure before they left." She looked at him disbelieving, thoughts racing. She shook her head slowly in disbelief. "What could they be looking for?"

"Maybe some proof they thought you found. Remember you were seen meeting with Hannah at her home."

Should she go home now? Was her sister safe? Then reality kicked in. Were 'they' trying to flush her out? Did it have something to do with her work with Wes or was it just a regular break-in by a regular thief? Were the police trying to contact her?

"What do I do now?" Wes came around to her side, and sat down next to her at the counter, quietly digesting the new information. He put his arm around her and gave her a warm hug.

"I'm not sure. We could call the police and tell them your neighbour called you, without telling them where you are of course."

"Maybe I could call my neighbour. She could maybe give me a bit more information. I could call …" Then she paused, "I, don't know what to do."

Wes took her hands in his. "I'll call Tony and ask him to take care of it. He can call the police, say he's your lawyer, tell them he heard from your neighbour, and that you are away on vacation. Then he can talk to your sister and explain." Tessa nodded in agreement, although she wanted to be home; to check for damage, to see if anything important was taken, but under the circumstances it seemed like a reasonable solution. Besides if something was stolen, she couldn't do

169

much about it other than make an insurance report when she returned.

Still worried, she smiled at his attempt to make her feel better. Without knowing who to trust, it was better not to involve anyone else now, and if Tony could deal with all the particulars; then that was probably the best way to handle things.

"I better call Tony, now." Before fishing his cell phone out of his pocket he handed her a piece of paper. "I'll use my cell phone, but first you better write your sister's name and number for me ... and your neighbour's too."

He was a while before coming back to the kitchen, but when he did, Wes looked relieved after speaking to his brother. "He said, he'd look after everything, and call your sister right away. I called Moose too and he'll see if he can find out more about the break-in."

Tessa had made tea while he was out of the room and she handed him a mug, that she had just poured. He smiled at her, glad now that they had some help. "The fire's good for another half hour or so, let's go down by the lake."

The tree line was barely visible against the darkness of the sky. The sky was cloudless allowing the light of the moon to reflect across the water in shimmering waves.

"We need to solve the '1881-n' message," Tessa said softly, her mind focused now on what needed to be done. "We need to prove that Alex Fenwick was Cyrus Griffin."

"We'll both work on that tomorrow, until we hear back from one of our sources." He smiled at a thought he just had. "Care to make a little wager as to which side finds something first."

She gave him a knowing look. "And, what did you have in mind."

He returned the look and revised his initial thought. "Breakfast … and … a shoulder massage?"

She smiled in response. "Make it a foot massage … and, you're on."

Chapter 19

It was early, Tessa rolled over, her head buried in her pillow. There was a noise she hadn't heard before; a thumping sound. Was Wes chopping wood? No, it was a hollow thump sound. She reached over to check the time—not quite seven. She felt the thump vibrate through her bed. Curious, she got her housecoat on, then went out into the hallway. Surprised, she found Wes crouched at the backdoor, watching whatever was making the sound. He turned and waved her to come over while putting a finger to his mouth, cautioning silence.

He was watching his Cruiser as it was being rocked by a very large black bear. They peered through the window of the storm door, the bear unaware of their presence. The bear, standing on his hind legs, was as tall as the vehicle and for some reason felt that moving it back and forth was accomplishing something.

"Maybe he smells some pasta left on the plate under the Cruiser." Wes shrugged, as if that was the only explanation he could think of.

"I doubt Herbert left a crumb on the plate, but the smell might still be there." She watched as the bear, frustrated, walked around the Cruiser, then slowly meandered around the yard before finally disappearing up the hill at the back of the road.

"Wow, wasn't that neat. I haven't seen him around before, but I'm glad he's gone now. I just hope he didn't scratch up the Cruiser too much." Wes seemed awed by the bears presence, and although she didn't admit it, Tessa was too. She'd never seen a bear up close before.

"Do you think he will come back? I'd hate for your grandmother to arrive home to a dangerous welcome."

"I think a moving car would probably scare him off, but I'll text Nan and let her know, just in case." He left the back door open with the storm-door window partially raised and went off in search of his cell phone. Tessa decided to get dressed. It would be a long day.

They shared the breakfast chores and by eight they were ready to look further into Keefer's mysterious text. "You mentioned yesterday we should look for lateral clues."

"Why don't you use newspapers.com while I look for anything on James Tyrell and his whereabouts after 1881, on the other sites," suggested Wes. The sky was cloudy with a grey shade that darkened the lake promising rain sometime soon. A drumming sound on the tree outside their window suggested that the woodpecker was back looking for grubs in the squirrel's tree.

Tessa stared at the screen waiting for a result to appear, then gave a short burst of surprise at finally finding something of importance. "Wes, I found him, I think." Wes leaned over to check out her findings as she read the newspaper.

"May 20th, 1881, The Exeter Flying Post. The apprehension of the Portsmouth murderer, James Tyrell, late of Knackers Knowle, has been accredited to constable Benjamin Taylor. Tyrell who is accused of smuggling, theft and willful murder, will be tried two weeks from today."

"That's very interesting. So, if it's the same James Tyrell, and by the address it appears it is, that means Alexander Fenwick's brother-in-law was a thief, a smuggler and apparently a murderer. I wonder if he got off?"

"Two weeks, is about June 3rd, so I'll look for more information."

"Wait, I saw something the other day when we started to look into Devon. You may have to look at the National Archives site. Here …" He switched back to the site he had saved—The Devon Heritage Centre. "It says that the more serious crimes were held by Assizes courts twice a year and …" He scrolled down reading the description. "The records are kept at the National Archives at Kew."

174

"Well, that's good to know for source information later," Tessa said, "but … I just found the juicy details. She turned the screen slightly so Wes could read the description of the trial from the newspaper Tessa had found.

According to the paper, James Tyrell had a small ship which he regularly used to smuggle anything that would bring him a profit. He had arranged to carry a Spaniard and his wife, to a specified landing area along the coast of Devon. The couple had two young girls with them, each in their early teens.

One of the girls, was later found by police after she escaped a brothel near Portsmouth. She told about the murder of the Spanish couple and how the first mate had sold her and her sister afterwards. She told too, that her guardians had brought with them a small chest of jewels and gold as a dowry from their parents. She described, how the Captain had argued with the Spaniard and wanted more money before delivering them to a safe landing place. Upon his refusal the two had fought resulting in the death of the couple.

The man and his wife had been found along the coast with their throats cut, their bodies afloat in the water near Portsmouth, with no sign of the metal box the girl had spoken of. As Captain, Tyrell and his first mate were held for the murder of the couple based on her testimony. The first mate, a man named Simpson, confessed he had taken the young women off the ship shortly after, at Tyrell's order. Tyrell had been tried June 4, 1881 and found guilty of murder. He was sentenced to hang. No mention of what happened to the box of jewels.

"I wonder what happened to the second girl?"

"Most likely disappeared. Probably sold. The sex trade was big even then."

"Didn't seem to bother the courts though, did it? That's sad."

Tessa extended her arms, giving them a stretch after sitting. "I wonder if the girl was returned to her parents? But, I suppose that's another story." She sighed, stifling a yawn. "I feel like having some tea, would you like some?"

"Thank you, yes." He waited until the noise of the water running ended once Tessa filled the kettle. "I was just thinking, what if Alexander got his hands on that missing box of jewels?"

Tessa leaned on the counter and contemplated the idea as the kettle heated. "They did live at the same address during this time," she offered. "Maybe the box was taken back to the house to hide until it was safe."

"You said, Cyrus Griffin was rich. What if he had help? What if he took the box of jewels, changed his name and hightailed it out of Dodge, so to speak? He had to leave fast and get far enough away, quickly, so he wouldn't be suspected."

The kettle whistled and Tessa poured the boiling water into a porcelain teapot. "And what better place to get rid of stolen goods, than in London." As the tea steeped, she prepared the two mugs, one with lots of milk and two sugars for herself, and one, black with one sugar for Wes.

She carried the mugs back to their table. "We could never prove it of course, but it makes sense. And it explains why he changed his name and left the baby behind. Who knows how much Alexander was involved with his brother-in-law's exploits?"

It was just after ten o'clock and the quiet was interrupted by the sound of a car coming up the laneway. Wes jumped up, hitting his foot on the table leg as he did. "Nan! I better make sure the bear is not still in the yard."

As it was, Nan had seen the bear further back on the road coming in, as it meandered back through the woods. She parked in her usual spot and waved a hello at Wes, who quickly went to escort her inside.

"Thanks for the warning, I've only ever seen a black bear once since moving here. He must have been looking for food."

"Probably, are you back to stay now?"

"Yes, my friend came home last night. She's doing much better and was glad to be back with her dogs." She pulled her small overnight bag from the passenger seat.

"Have you had breakfast yet?" He asked as he held the door open for her.

"Yes, but I wouldn't mind a cup of tea."

"You're just in time, Tessa just made a pot."

They sat around the kitchen counter as Tessa and Wes told Nan of their recent discoveries.

A musical tone rang interrupting their conversation. Tessa sat on the counter side closest to the living room. "Is that your cell phone?"

Wes's hand automatically went to his jeans pocket. "Yes, it's over by the computer. I'll get it."

Realizing too, it might be one of her detectives Tessa made a run to get it before Wes could reach it. "Not if I reach it first." They scrambled to get to the phone first in a fit of laughter and giggles. He tried to hold her back, his arm around her waist. Her hand grabbed the phone a second before Wes could reach it. "Yes? It's me, Neal," she said out of breath. "What did you find?" She smiled triumphantly at Wes, then started to scribble down notes as she listened. "Great work, we'll check it out. Keep looking." She put the phone down where she had found it and turned around to face two expectant faces.

"That was Neal. He's found a Jerry Ainsley in a group home near a place called Smiths Falls, Ontario. He thinks it might be our guy as the age fits a possible son of Jeremy Ainsley but doesn't know anything else about him." She walked slowly back to the counter happy now that they seemed to be making some progress. Wes put the phone back in his pocket then followed her back, giving her a hug in passing at their mutual success. "How far is Smiths Falls?"

"Maybe … three hours." He read the note she had hastily written noting the address. "When do you want to leave."

"We'll need a place to stay. I can look for something on the internet first." Tessa checked the time. It was just after eleven. "In an hour?"

"Good, I'll get ready."

Chapter 20

The grey from earlier had lightened somewhat but still covered the sky with a low cloud making the drive a pleasant one, without the sun glaring through the S.U.V. windows. Wes had plugged the address into his navigational device, and they were now approaching the town of Perth. The group home was between Perth and Smiths Falls just a few more minutes away. Tessa had booked two rooms at an Inn close by, and it was there they stopped first before going on to find Jerry Ainsley. It was almost four o'clock by the time they reached the group home.

The building was brick, three stories and lots of windows which had the look of a school from the 1940s, only the metal grates over the windows indicated this building had a different purpose.

They parked in the visitor section of the parking lot and sat in the Cruiser before getting out, deciding what their story would be once inside and face to face with the administrator. After discussing a few scenarios, Tessa agreed that they should, be as honest as possible about their hunt for a long lost relative—leaving out the millions in inheritance that might belong to this resident.

The administrator or director as she called herself was a Miss Helen Randolph. A woman in her mid forties, she had looked after this home for almost fifteen years. A tall, erect woman, she gave the appearance of having been in the military, a fact confirmed by a photograph on her desk.

After showing their credentials, Wes and Tessa explained their visit. "So, you see, Miss Randolph, our client hired us to search for Mr. Ainsley. If indeed he, is related to Jeremy Ainsley, he would be the last of her family."

Miss Randolph sat behind a large oak desk—her back facing, it seemed, the only unbarred window on the building—and pondered their request for a moment.

"I'm afraid there's not a lot I can tell you about Mr. Ainsley." She adjusted her glasses as she looked at the file, she had pulled from her filing cabinet. She smiled as she checked the notes made by the previous administrator. "Luckily for your investigation, Jerry is not a resident; where rules as a patient would prevail, but a volunteer who needed a place to live." She turned the scant number of pages in the file. "There is a brief explanation, here." She read the page as if for the first time.

Apparently, Jeremy Ainsley had arrived with an old army friend many years ago, who had been admitted with advanced Alzheimer's. Jeremy Ainsley had no place to go and stayed on as a kitchen volunteer. He had been the home's cook for many years until he too became impaired with dementia. Now he lived at the home helping with smaller chores he was still able to do.

"As to family, I have never met any and he has never spoken of any, and no one to my knowledge has ever visited him." She laid the file down with a finality that suggested there was nothing more she could tell them. "Seeing he is not technically a 'patient' there's no reason why you can't speak with him, but I will have to ask him first."

She stood abruptly indicating the meeting had concluded. "If you would please wait in the living room across the hall." She waved a hand in the general direction of the living room.

The living room had a wide screen television, a fireplace, several card tables set with various games and puzzles, and many chairs and couches where residents could congregate and socialize.

At this moment Wes and Tessa were the only two enjoying the large room. It wasn't long before the administrator was back with a young attendant at her side. She smiled at the two visitors. Annie will take you up to his room

He's eager to meet you.

They were escorted by elevator to the third floor, then to a room where the door had been left open.

Tessa's eyes widened as Jeremy Ainsley turned to look at them as they entered his room. The pale blue eyes, and the peppered-grey hair, could have been those of Hannah Wentworth, but unlike Hannah, Jeremy had a deep scar across this forehead and seemed quite frail.

He smiled when he saw his visitors. They sat on two folding chairs that the attendant had brought into the room for their visit. His small apartment was really only one room, bedroom and living room combined with a small bathroom off to the side. Jeremy sat in his recliner next to the bed, a pale blue recliner, that brought back moments of another blue chair for Tessa.

There were some photos sitting on the side table between his bed and chair under a tall lamp. One of a family; possibly his wife with two small children. Another of a soldier in his uniform, and a third of two soldiers laughing as they shared a meal under a camouflage net.

"Hello, Mr. Ainsley, my name is Tessa, and this is Wes. We're looking for a Jeremy Ainsley who used to live in England. Do you know where your father was born?" He smiled and seemed eager to participate in the conversation. Unlike Hannah though, it didn't take long for Tessa to realize he had lost all grasp of reality.

"Fred and I went on a ship once." He reached over and picked up the picture of the two soldiers. He smiled at the memory of long ago. He lives here, you know." Tessa glanced at the attendant, who had decided to remain in the room. She shook her head, and closed her eyes slowly, indicating that Fred no longer was alive except in Jerry's mind.

"It must be nice to have a good friend like that," Wes suggested. Jerry nodded in agreement. Wes was more interested in the framed picture of the family on the table. "Is this your family?" It was a small, square, coloured, photograph, the clothing and hairstyles reminiscent of the 1970's. "May I look at them."

Eager for the attention, the frail man handed Wes the picture. "Do you know them?" he asked.

Not knowing how to answer, Wes smiled at the two young children—probably five and seven years old—happy as they opened their Christmas presents. "They are very beautiful." The back of the frame had a cardboard backing that slid into place. Wes gently pulled it free, sliding it up so he could see the back of the picture. 'Alice and the kids, 1979.'

"This is Alice," he said, handing the photograph back to the elderly man. "Do you remember Alice?"

Jerry Ainsley held the picture, contemplating the figures from long ago. His eyes stared at the them without recognition. "Alice?"

"Yes, her name is Alice."

"She's very lovely." His eyes closed slowly; the visitors forgotten.

"He's tired," said the attendant. "Thank you for coming to visit."

The visit ended, Wes and Tessa quietly left, as the attendant covered Jerry's lap with a blanket.

Once outside, Tessa made some notes as they sat in the car. "What a sweet guy. It's too bad he couldn't help us more."

"I was just hoping he could name his family. The kids must be in their forties by now. It doesn't seem as if they visited him."

"Hard to say, if his mind is going. Well, we did learn something. Because his friend Fred is deceased, we were able to get his last name from the administrator. And because he is a deceased soldier, maybe his name is in the war records we searched earlier. If he is, we can get some of Jerry's military information. They had to have been in the same unit."

Wes leaned back in the driver's seat and reached for his seatbelt. "We've forgotten one important thing."

Tessa clicked her seat belt into position. "What's that?"

"We don't know if this Jerry Ainsley, is the person we're looking for, and even if he is, do you suppose Hannah's lawyer would agree to hand over millions to him?"

"Probably not. So, we have to find some proof either way." A small fly crawled up the glass of her window and she stopped in thought to roll it down so the insect could escape. "He seemed like a very kind man; I hope he had a good life. Did you notice the scar on his forehead? I wonder if that affected his memory."

"Probably, no telling though, how or where he got it." Wes started the car. "He must be getting a pension cheque each month. They'd have records of his age of course. The census records, if they were available could tell us where he was born."

"They must allow judges or lawyers to see a census record of a person if it were important?"

"Now, that I don't know, but we can certainly ask Tony."

The car had been running and now the air conditioning had replaced the hot stuffy air. "Back to the Inn?"

186

"Let's stop at a store first and get a few things to snack on for later."

Chapter 21

They sat by a window enjoying the scenery during their supper, the inn was built on the edge of a wooded area and provided the guests with a pleasant relaxing view while they ate. Wes was reading the answer to a text message he had sent Tony. "He says, that no one can look at a census record except the person on the record, unless they are deceased. An unwell person could have access if his power of attorney asks on his behalf, and we found out from Miss Randolph that Jerry Ainsley doesn't seem to have a power of attorney."

The waitress brought their food, the first they'd had since leaving the cottage. Wes looked at the large steak on his plate, complete with baked potato and vegetables. Then he looked at Tessa's plate, just as full but with pan fried fish and salad.

Tessa, looked at her meal. "Wow, I didn't realize how hungry I was." The waitress came back with a carafe of wine which Wes quickly poured into their glasses. "Thank you." They clinked glasses before starting to eat.

"This is nice." She waved her hand encompassing their surroundings, her fork still holding a piece of fish.

The inn itself was very traditional and incorporated a

great deal of wood and antiques attempting to give a nineteenth-century atmosphere. Their dining room gave off an ambience of romance. Each table dimly lit with candle light. Wall sconces lined the area along the dining tables further giving off a warm glow. Outside a few trees closest to the inn had been decorated with mini lights, their soft illumination casting shadows along the edge of the woods.

She finished her bite of fish. "The food is good too."

Focused again on their hunt, she said, "So, I guess we have no choice but to look for his wife Alice, and the kids." Then a thought occurred to her. "If Alice Ainsley is dead that means we can look for her on a 1961 or '71 census, doesn't it?"

"True, but I'm sure too that all other names would be blackened out. I think we better ask our helpers to start looking through city directories for possible children." He took a bite of his steak and sighed in exaggerated bliss. "Oh, this is so good," he said, then added, "What did you say Jeremy Ainsley's father's name was? The one in England."

"Mark, Mark Ainsley. Why, do you think Jeremy followed the tradition and named his son after his father?"

"It's a place to start."

She'd put her hair up, held by a pewter clip with a Celtic design she had found in an Irish shop close by the grocery store they had visited earlier. An escaped strand of hair had escaped and hung in a wave along side her cheek. Then he wondered if it was meant to be like that and smiled. The candle light flickered with the movement of others in the room giving her face a soft golden glow, her blue eyes now a deep navy. He thought she was beautiful and wanted to tell her but instead smiled as they ate their meal. Something she said interrupted his thoughts.

"Is that a wolf?" Something outside had caught her attention.

He looked where her fork pointed. "It looks like a fox, from its size."

"I've never seen a fox before."

"There's quite a few at Nan's place, but I haven't seen one this close up for a while."

The fox wandered close to the dining room windows, as if curious about the creatures that sat inside. The couple behind them stood up to leave, their movement noticed through the window; and the fox was just as quickly gone, back to the woods that were its home.

"Just as well," said Wes. "It's the cautious ones that

stay alive." Tessa nodded and resumed her meal.

Tessa took a sip of her wine and watched Wes as he poured more into her glass, then his own. "There doesn't seem to be any records we can look up, not unless the person is deceased."

Wes agreed. "Let's hope we can find a relative, but if Jeremy Ainsley was sent to another country, we might have to give up the search. It may take years and I'm afraid Fairchild's discovery will probably go unchallenged."

"Our job is to find missing people. We do it every day, so I won't give up," insisted Tessa. "Even if I have to hire a professional genealogist and start over. There has to be something we don't know how to find. Maybe our guys can find a death for Jeremy Ainsley."

The waitress came by and cleared away their plates while offering them a dessert menu.

"Would you care for some dessert?" He took the proffered folders and handed one to Tessa.

"No, I'm just pleasantly full."

He smiled at the waitress and handed back the dessert menus. "Just the bill, please."

"My treat," he added, when he saw Tessa reach for her bag.

"Let's give it until tomorrow. I know we can both work better from our own offices." He wondered if 'they' had given up looking for Tessa, and decided not to take a chance. "I think we better find another place for you to stay until we're finished, just to be safe."

"What about my place? I have to go back and see if anything was taken."

Wes nodded in compliance. "Then we go together, just in case it's being watched."

Their rooms were on the second floor, next to each other. "Nine, tomorrow?" she asked fumbling for the key in her bag. She found the key, but before placing it in the lock, Wes turned her slightly and put his arms around her. Tessa hugged him back and laid her head against his chest. She could hear his heart beat through the thin denim and smiled.

"As difficult as this has been, I've enjoyed every minute. I'll have to thank Duffy when I see him." He stepped back enough to disengage the hug and took her face in his hands. His lips engulfed hers in a slow passionate kiss. Her arms wrapped around him again as she returned the passion.

After several moments in a romantic embrace, she suddenly felt awkward when another couple walked past them grinning, as they walked down the hall to their own room.

"Hmmmmm…" She smiled up at Wes. "You know … you still owe me a foot massage."

Wes had heard the couple behind him and waited until their door had closed. "Your room or mine?"

"She gave him a knowing look. "Well, since I have my key."

She unlocked her door just as a musical interlude suggested someone was calling on Wes's phone. He gave a sigh, then quickly pulled the phone out of his jeans pocket and answered the call.

"Hello? Yes. What have you got?" Tessa waited patiently as Wes talked to one of his detectives. "Okay, send me a text with name, address and phone number for each one. We can start tomorrow. Okay, then send the times. Good work!"

He smiled triumphantly at the new lead. "Mike found four people who fit out profile and might have a connection to either the Jerry Ainsley we found, or maybe another one."

The foot massage forgotten for the moment; Tessa felt exalted at the prospects of finding potential relatives of Hannah's. "You really feel that Jeremy Ainsley came to Ontario before the war, don't you?"

"I know it's a long shot, but I do. A father who cared

enough about his son to see him safe away from the bombing, I'm sure would make the effort to send him to the safety of the boy's grandfather. And Mark Ainsley must have known that Jeremy Fenwick was here in Ontario."

"I hope your right. It still doesn't mean that the Jerry Ainsley we found at the home is related to the child who came over in 1938, but it's a place to start looking for Jeremy Fenwick's grandson, I suppose."

"It is, and tomorrow we head to …" He checked the text message that had just been sent, "Ottawa, to meet a Mark Ainsley. Mike will arrange the interviews and send the times to us tomorrow. He'll try to arrange the times so we don't have to back track."

Chapter 22

Tessa compared the address she had written quickly on a piece of paper, with the street map shown on the screen of Wes's navigational device. "Turn right at the next light." she said, confident they were going the right way. Last night they had discussed their plan of attack. Wes had suggested that they continue to be as honest as possible without mentioning Hannah's name or the amount of any potential inheritance. To mention Hannah Wentworth's name might jeopardize the responses of the people they wanted to talk to, if they'd watched the news recently, and to discuss millions might further complicate the truthfulness of their statements. Luckily each of the four people were receptive to speaking with them, resulting in their first appointment in Ottawa—Mr. Mark Ainsley.

"Next street on the left." She checked the homes looking for a number on one of the buildings for further reference. "It'll be up ahead on the right."

They parked on the road in front the Ainsley home. Tessa had listed some of the questions they would ask without appearing too desperate or intrusive, and put her note pad in her bag before waving a 'hello' to the lady on the front porch.

"Thank you, for seeing us," Tessa said after introducing Wes as her partner. Tessa noticed Mrs. Ainsley had prepared a portion of her front porch for the interview, and they dutifully sat at the proffered chairs.

"I'm sorry my husband couldn't be here; he's in Calgary with my son." She smiled proudly. "He's starting a new job there this fall. He's moving there with his wife and children once he can find a home to rent. He has two boys, fifteen and twelve." She poured some iced tea for each of them, then sat back in her whicker chair. "I hope I might be of some assistance." So, her son was around forty, which would make Mrs. Ainsley probably in her mid sixties.

Wes explained the reason for their visit. "We were hired by an elderly lady who is trying to find the last of her family before she dies." That was as straight forward as he could make it.

"Her cousin's name is, or was, Jeremy Ainsley. He was born in England and we think he came to Canada around 1938."

"Ahh," she said. "Then I might be of little help. I've never met Mark's father, but I do know my husband was very insistent when our son was born that we stick to the family name. That's why we named our son Mark Ainsley. My

196

husband's father and grandfather were both named Mark and he wanted to continue the tradition. As to where he was born, I can't say, but perhaps my husband will know.

There first interview cut short by this admission Tessa and Wes politely carried on with the conversation, outlining a bit of their search, before thanking Mrs. Ainsley for her assistance and time.

Once back in the Cruiser, Tessa checked for the next appointment. "One down, and three to go."

"Where to now?"

"Mississauga."

They followed the 401 Highway west, then took the Hurontario exit. It was another twenty minutes to the growing community of Meadowvale on the west side of Mississauga.

Jeremy Ainsley seemed in his late twenties. Tall, fair-haired with light blue eyes. He welcomed them but confessed he'd suddenly been called into work at the hospital and didn't have much time to discuss their errand.

"Have a seat." He offered them the couch as he took an opposite chair. They introduced themselves and briefly explained their reason for visiting.

He leaned back, thinking. "I wish I could ask my father some of your questions." He looked down and paused before continuing. "My parents were killed when I was little ... car accident. I was raised by my dad's sister; Aunt Liz. We never talked about the family much. I remember her telling me once, that her father abandoned their family when they were little. Her mother died quite young of cancer." He smiled weakly. "I'm afraid that's all I know."

Tessa had been taking some brief notes as he spoke. Wes nodded in understanding. "Did your Aunt ever mention her father's name."

Jeremy Ainsley shook his head slightly. "It wasn't something we ever spoke of ... there was a great deal of hurt." He glanced at the living room wall clock, then stood up abruptly. "I'm sorry," he said, "but I really have to leave now or I'll be late."

Wes shook his hand. "That's perfectly alright. We thank you for seeing us on such short notice."

It was starting to get late and they hadn't had supper yet, but there were two more people to meet—one in Hamilton and the last one in Beamsville—as long as their detective didn't call with more names.

Jerry Ainsley, there Hamilton appointment, was in his late sixties according to Mike's notes but the man whom they met on an eight-foot ladder cleaning the eaves troughs seemed in excellent condition and could easily be taken for forty.

Jerry Ainsley was a pleasant man, though not a natural conversationalist as Tessa and Wes discovered. He did however give adequate answers to their questions.

He'd grown up in Ontario. His father would have been close to ninety, had he not died two years ago. And Jerry Ainsley was indeed named after his father, Gerald Ainsley— Jerry for short.

Their interview had lasted a brief twenty minutes, after which Tessa and Wes had driven away, a bit disappointed. They had driven around the block then parked along the curb as they sat and contemplated their next move.

It was getting late and it was cutting it close to the last interview time. "I'll call and let them know where we are and see if it's still okay to come by."

It was almost seven o'clock as they crossed the Burlington Skyway. The highway traffic was busy but not as busy as the usual rush hour delays, which helped their timeline. Tessa checked the navigation screen. "We get off at Ontario Street, Beamsville, then take the service road to Mountainview Road."

It was Mrs. Ainsley who answered the door when they pressed the doorbell. She was a tall woman and fair of colouring, and her accent betrayed her Swedish birth. The door entrance opened up into a living room where Mr. Ainsley sat in his wheelchair. Mr. and Mrs. Jeremy Ainsley were welcoming and seemed happy to have some company, despite the hour. After the preliminaries, the four sat together in front of the living room coffee table laden with some muffins, cookies and tea that she had prepared for their visit. The Ainsleys were retired and in their late sixties. Jeremy Ainsley knew a lot about his father. His name too was Jeremy. He had been born in Britain, although he wasn't sure of the place. He had died in 2006, at the age of 85, which meant that this Jeremy Ainsley, his father, was born in 1921, several years different than the Jeremy Ainsley they were seeking. But memory make mistakes, and it was definitely something they could check out in the British registers.

The visit was informative, and Tessa was hopeful now that they might have found their connection to Jeremy Ainsley—the son of Sarah and Mark Ainsley, the grandson of Cyrus Griffin. She was glad too that the couple had three children, all of whom lived in Canada. Promising to keep in touch and let them know the results of their findings, Wes and Tessa left.

"I think I'd like to go home now and check on my

house. Do you think it's safe?"

Wes contemplated her request. "It's been a while since the break-in, maybe we can chance it. We can keep the lights off."

"That shouldn't matter, I always keep a light on in the living room using a timer. We can keep to the back of the house."

He took her hand in his. "Okay, let's do that then," he said, then started the Cruiser. "So, it's off to St. Catharines."

With the traffic, it took another hour and a half to get to Tessa's house. They parked on a near-by street then followed along the grassy ravine that joined the back yards of Tessa's neighbours. There was still some light left which made the path way to Mary's house easy to see.

After telling her friend Mary that she had arrived home, Wes and Tessa entered her house through the back door. There was a faint glow of light from the front of the house, but it was only the lamp that Tessa had put on a timer.

Nothing looked disturbed as they came into the family room from the back sunroom. It was after dark now, but the glow of the night sky allowed them some light. The vertical blinds were partially open, but Tessa kept to the sides of the room out of view of the front window. She glanced quickly around. All of her electronical equipment was where she had left it, but drawers in her desk had been opened and dumped. She moved along the wall and entered the single bedroom of the small home. It was dark and her bed and dresser were shadows, but she could tell by the dark lumps of clothing on the floor that the thief had searched this room as well. Her jewellery box had been turned over with its contents –mostly costume jewellery—now on the floor.

Wes had waited for her in the family room. "What do you think, is anything missing?"

She joined him, then smiled. "I don't think so, but whoever it was, searched the place pretty good."

"But there's one place he didn't search." She left the room and headed for the kitchen, Wes following. Tessa went straight to the fridge and removed a jar of mayonnaise. She held it out for him to see smiling in triumph.

"It's a good thing he didn't stop to make a sandwich." She unscrewed the lid and dumped the contents on the kitchen counter top, revealing gold rings, necklaces and the pendant Hannah had given her among them. Wes picked up the mayonnaise jar checking the inside. "I saw that on the internet," she said proudly. "You take an empty jar, I guess it could be anything really, even peanut butter. Anyway, you paint the inside of the jar the same colour as the stuff that used to be in it, and voila, you have a safe place to keep valuables. I usually put my extra jewellery in here if I know I will be away for a while."

"Wow, the things you can learn on the internet." He looked around for the bag of fried chicken dinners they had picked up on their way home from Beamsville. He looked inside the open fridge for something to drink. "I'm glad nothing of value was taken." He'd found a bottle of unopened white wine in the fridge door and pulled it out of the compartment. Looking through the upper cupboards for two glasses, he paused at Tessa's gasp.

"Oh, my God. Wes, I've had it all along … the proof. This is what the thief was searching for." She sat down, her hands starting to shake.

He stopped his search and took her hands in his to calm her. "Okay, what do you mean proof."

"DNA—proof. Here, in the back"—she held out the locket for him to see—"is a lock of Cyrus Griffin's hair. It can be used to identify the heir to Hannah's money. Don't you see, they knew I had it." She looked around, as if expecting the thief to spring from a corner of the room.

Wes handled the locket, contemplating their next move.

"I'll call Tony and let him know. He can call your sister too and let her know everything is okay." He handled the gold keepsake. "This is the link we need to prove Alexander Fenwick and Cyrus Griffin were one in the same. He scooped up her jewellery along with the locket and dropped them back inside the fake jar of mayonnaise. "For now, I think we should keep this in the fridge, where it will be safe. That is unless another thief comes along and decides to stop and make a sandwich." He gave a faint snort at the thought of that image then gave Tessa a hug.

"We've got one potential Jeremy Ainsley." Just as he had finished the sentence his cell phone rang. "Hello? Yes." Then he handed Tessa the phone. "It's for you."

"Yes, just a minute while I get something to write with." Wes fumbled in his pocket then handed her a pen. There was the paper bag containing their supper, so he tore off a piece and gave it to her.

She wrote quickly, then thanked her caller. "That was Chelsey. She's found a woman by the name of Alice Ainsley whose father was Jeremy Ainsley."

"Where?"

"Niagara Falls."

Chapter 23

Wes licked the last remnants of chicken coating from his fingers and then gave them a good wipe on a piece of dampened paper towel. They sat on the floor, on cushions using the coffee table for their dining, a small candle allowing just enough light to see by. "That was tasty."

"It's been a while since I've had fried chicken. The french fries weren't too bad considering they sat in their box for a while."

Wes nodded. "It's hard to spoil french fries," he said, then reconsidered, "unless they're cold from the fridge."

She smiled at the face he made. "Having the microwave does help." She wiped her hands and with her glass of wine in hand took up a place on the couch. Wes joined her and they sat back relaxed after a day of disappointment and hope.

"What time tomorrow do we see Alice Ainsley?"

"Noon. Tessa took a sip of wine then contemplated this new person. "Do you think she's related to the Jerry we met in the home?"

"Well, the name is unusual for today, so maybe she was named after Jerry's wife Alice. We'll have to wait and see." He scooted a bit closer to Tessa inviting her to lean against him, which she did. He leaned over and gave her a kiss that lasted longer than he'd hoped.

Tessa smiled at him. He looked very handsome in the candlelight. His dark hair hung down over his forehead, his eyes bright with expectation. Then a thought occurred to her. "What was the name of Jeremy Ainsley's step mother. The one his father Mark married shortly after Sarah died."

Wes's mind was a bit fuzzy, but he had found that information back at the cottage and remembered the record. "Elizabeth, Elizabeth Kirkland, why?"

"I just got thinking about the young man who was raised by his Aunt. Liz is usually short for Elizabeth isn't it? If our Jeremy Ainsley was a baby when his mother Sarah died, he would have thought of Elizabeth as his mother."

Wes was following along. "So, you think we should speak to Jeremy's Aunt Liz?"

"I don't think we should rule it out … you never know."

"True, we should follow all leads. Here, lean back." He fluffed one of the couch pillows and placed it on his lap so Tessa could rest her head. He smiled as he stroked back her hair from her face, her blue eyes watching him.

"I was just thinking of Keefer. Do you think they will find the car that killed him, or the driver?"

"I don't know, maybe, one day. We may never know how or why it happened. Whether it was deliberate or an accident, or who sent the message he was typing. Or what happened to his phone."

"I think when our work is done, I will go and visit his family," said Tessa.

There was the familiar ring of his phone. "Sorry." He nudged her slightly as he retrieved it. "Hello? Hi, Moose. When?" He waited as Moose explained, Tessa's eyes hopeful that Moose had found the Jeremy Ainsley they were seeking. "Have they made any arrests? Okay, thanks."

One of your neighbours had some security footage of the guy who broke into your house. Moose went around and explained the situation and found that the guy across the street had some video of the thief getting out of a car just past his driveway. It showed the licence plate and Moose was able to find out who owned the car." He paused keeping Tessa in suspense.

"Okay, who owned it? Thanks, keep me updated."

"It was a rental car, rented by Fairchild's law firm. There've been no arrests because you can't clearly see the person driving. And your neighbour didn't happen to be watching your house at the time so in theory it could just have been an innocent visitor, but the connection is there." Wes checked his watch. "It's getting late, and we've had a long day." He patted the couch. "This will be fine for me; you better get a good night's sleep."

Tired and feeling relaxed from the wine, Tessa reluctantly sat up. "There're blankets in this cupboard."

Wes followed her to the hall. He chose a couple from the shelf then turned to give her a hug and kiss good night. "See you in the morning."

Niagara Falls was only twenty minutes away, and with the highway near her home, it was easy to find Alice Ainsley's home on Dorchester Road. "Three houses up, on the right."

They parked on the road, as the small driveway had its limit of vehicles, and Tessa hoped they weren't intruding. She checked the time on the dash; it was noon. Once at the door they could hear several voices coming from the living room, women's voices. The door opened as she was about to knock, and they were greeted by a petite woman, possibly in her mid-forties. She glanced over her shoulder at the group of young women gathered in the next room.

"Come in, don't mind the noise." She held the screen

door for Tessa and Wes as they entered the home. It seemed a joyous occasion. "My daughter is getting married, and her friends are here to help her choose the décor and the venue." She walked them past the happy bride to be and went into the dining room area.

She invited them to sit. "Now, the young lady on the phone said you were inquiring about my father." She spoke quickly and seemed to want to rejoin the decision making in the other room, so Tessa shortened their introductions and then came to the point of the visit.

"Our colleague mentioned to us that your father Jeremy Ainsley is named after your grandfather." Tessa glanced back at the young women and suddenly realized they might have the wrong person, maybe it was her husband they should talk to.

Alice Ainsley picked up on Tessa's confusion then clarified. "Ainsley is my maiden name," she said. "I divorced my husband four years ago, then returned to my own name … so yes my father is Jeremy Ainsley. But you're wrong about his name, he's named after his grandfather, not mine—Jeremy Woodburn, his mother's father."

She saw Wes nod his head in understanding. "Does that make a difference?" she asked.

"I'm afraid it does, for us," said Tessa. "You see we're

looking for Jeremys descended from the Ainsley line." There was a shriek of excitement in the adjoining room and Tessa felt badly for taking Alice Ainsley away from her daughter. "I'm sorry, I'm afraid we've wasted your time."

"That's perfectly all right, I was just hoping I'd be of some help to you." At that, she shook Tessa's hand then escorted them to the front door. "I hope you find the person you're looking for."

They sat in their car contemplating their last lead. Liz Ainsley was unmarried and lived alone on a small property in the town of Innisfil, south of Barrie. They had been able to get her address and phone number from her nephew and had been invited to see her at four o'clock.

Wes checked the time. It was now twelve-thirty barring traffic jams or accidents, they had enough time to get to their next meeting. It was a pleasant, late summer afternoon a bit warmer than it had been which required the air conditioning.

They arrived at the town of Innisfil with a half hour to spare. They stopped at a gas station to fill up while Tessa went inside and asked directions for Purvis Street. Another ten minutes and they had found the home of Liz Ainsley, an older home that had the look of a cottage from earlier days. Wood logs covered the exterior, but whether it was siding meant to replicate actual logs of days gone by, Tessa couldn't tell. She knocked at the front door while Wes re-parked the Cruiser to allow an electrical crew on the street, enough room to work. She knocked again as Wes joined her at the door. "Nobody home?" he asked, glancing in the sidelight beside the door.

A voice hailed them from the side of the house, "Hello. Are you Tessa?"

"Yes, I'm afraid we're a little early. Is that all right?"

"Certainly." She shook their hands in turn then gestured they follow her to the back yard of her home which overlooked Lake Simcoe. "We might as well enjoy the day. The lake is quite calm today."

Liz Ainsley had arranged some deck chairs around a central wooden table for their visit. There were glasses, a wine bottle, a decanter of what appeared to be iced tea, and slices of pound cake. She passed them each a glass and bade them to please help themselves. Wes looked at Tessa with an impish grin. "You're driving, right?" She smiled and nodded, which meant only one of them could have the wine, so he reached over and poured himself half a glass while she chose the tea.

"Jeremy called me last night to say you were looking for another Jeremy Ainsley, who would be around ninety years old now." The woman was tall and quite slim. Her eyes were a light blue, and Tessa suddenly felt she was looking at a younger version of Hannah Wentworth. She was in her mid-forties and lived alone along the shores of this beautiful lake. The easel set up between the pines at the edge of the lake indicated her profession.

"I'm afraid I don't know a great deal about my father other than his name." She looked down as if embarrassed by what she would tell them next. Tessa also saw a tinge of regret. "He abandoned our family when I was about four, I think. Mother never spoke of him often after that, I think she knew it was for the better. I do remember the fighting and arguing."

Wes glanced at Tessa and asked their first question. "What was your mother's name."

She looked puzzled because she knew they were looking for a Jeremy Ainsley. "Alice, why?" She smiled remembering her mother. "Her name was Alice MacDonald."

Tessa touched her hand and smiled. "I think we know where your father is and possibly why he left your family."

She sat silently, as Wes and Tessa told her about the Jerry Ainsley they had met in the group home. How he had been in the Vietnam War and somehow had suffered a head

212

injury, whether from war or accident they couldn't say, but it might have affected his behaviour. They told her about the picture on his night stand, the picture of a wife named Alice and a forgotten family.

Her eyes glazed with emotion. "All this time, he was so close by. If only I'd known." She wiped a moistened cheek.

Tessa renewed her glass of tea, giving Liz a moment to compose herself. "I don't suppose you know very much about your grandfather then."

She shook her head slightly. "No. As I said, mother never talked about my father or his family after he left. I only know he was English." Tessa gave Wes a hopeful glance. "My brother might have known more, but as you know he's gone now." Then her eyes brightened with an idea, I have a few of my mother's papers, I've kept them for my nephew just in case he might want to have them someday."

She left briefly and returned through the back door with a small brown envelope. She smiled as she opened the flap. "It's been so long since I last saw these, I'm afraid I no longer remember what's inside." She slipped the contents out onto the table, then opened the first of two folded papers. She glanced at it reading the top line before passing it to Tessa. "This is my mother's birth certificate, but I don't suppose it will be of much help."

Tessa read the information before passing it to Wes. Alice MacDonald was born in Buffalo, New York, in 1950. The second document was slightly torn where it had been folded, as if it had been read many times then refolded after each. "This is my mother's marriage certificate."

"They must have been happy then. I'd forgotten they were married in New York." She passed it carefully to Tessa. "Is Cattaraugus any where near Niagara Falls? It would have been nice if they honeymooned there."

"I'm sorry, I don't know." Tessa passed the paper to Wes and gave him a look that suggested he read it carefully. "Look." She waited quietly as Wes checked the certificate with a practiced eye. Liz had noticed the look between the two and watched as Wes read the document.

Wes smiled at both women, and Tessa squeezed his hand, as he read aloud the information recorded about the groom's father. Jeremy Ainsley, occupation—printer. "Miss Liz, I have one question for you?"

She nodded slightly, her eyes questioning, still not understanding.

"Would you be willing to take a DNA test?" It was now that Wes and Tessa explained the possible inheritance of

Hannah Wentworth. Liz was shocked and after a moment digesting the information she smiled and nodded.

"This will be wonderful for Jeremy, if it's true. He works so hard."

Wes and Tessa left Liz hopeful and excited.

After they left Liz Ainsley, they went to a nearby fast-food restaurant and sat in the car before going in to order. They were both elated at having found potential heirs—Hannah's family.

"I need to call Tony and get him going on this. We need to present our findings to a judge before any DNA testing, and we shouldn't disturb the locket until an expert at DNA has it to test."

"Do you think Liz will go and visit her father?" Tessa hoped she would.

"I don't know. I'd like to think so."

"What about the lawyer. Do you think he will persist with his suddenly found heir."

"I doubt it, now that we have the DNA to compare potential descendants with Cyrus Griffin. Duffy will swear to the authenticity of the locket, so if they test positive, I'm sure the courts will award them fairly." He sighed at the choices displayed on the board above the store. "And don't forget all the work we did in proving the Alexander Fenwick and Cyrus Griffin were one in the same."

Tessa pulled the note pad from her bag. "That reminds me, I now have a final chart to complete." She added the last of the names needed to fulfill Hannah's family.

"Good. So, what now?"

"I suppose we eat, drive home and renew our lives on Monday. I have another case I have to start on."

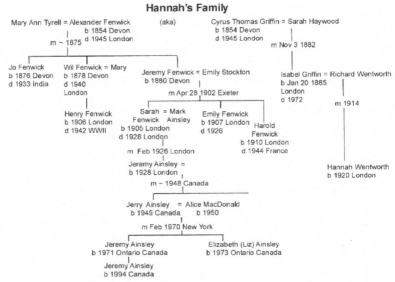

He gave her a shy glance. "I mean what about us?"

Tessa smiled and gave him a knowing look. "Well, I suppose we eat, drive home … and then, I get my foot massage."

Jacqueline Opresnik lives in Ontario, Canada,
with her husband Frank and Bengal cat Tiggy.
She received her degree in mathematics and
geology from Brock University.
She earned her pilot's licence shortly after, where
she met her husband. Jackie pursued a teaching
career and taught in the elementary grades.
She has had a love of writing since she was ten and
is just now beginning to fulfill her dreams
as an author.

Made in the USA
Coppell, TX
07 September 2021